I0641998

T. W. Rollestone

Life of Gotthold Ephraim Lessing

T. W. Rollestone

Life of Gotthold Ephraim Lessing

ISBN/EAN: 9783743333680

Manufactured in Europe, USA, Canada, Australia, Japa

Cover: Foto ©Raphael Reischuk / pixelio.de

Manufactured and distributed by brebook publishing software (www.brebook.com)

T. W. Rollestone

Life of Gotthold Ephraim Lessing

LIFE

OF

GOTTHOLD EPHRAIM LESSING.

BY

T. W. ROLLESTON

———

LONDON
WALTER SCOTT, 24, WARWICK LANE
1889

NOTE.

A LL the sources from which the materials for this account of Lessing's life have been drawn cannot be conveniently enumerated here ; but among those which have been of special use to me, I may mention the biographies of Heinrich Düntzer and Erich Schmidt, and the critical studies of Kuno Fischer and Victor Cherbuliez.

To the English biographies of Mr. James Sime and Miss Helen Zimmern my thanks are also due, if this work shall be judged, within its own narrower limits, to be not unworthy of these predecessors.

T. W. R.

CONTENTS.

LIFE OF LESSING.

CHAPTER I.

EXCEPT for Luther's great translation of the Bible,
and some valiant and pious Protestant hymns, the
Reformation in Germany, fruitful as it was in the field
of politics, was long sterile in that of literature. How
could it be otherwise? In soil scathed by the light-
nings of the Thirty Years' War with all its widespread,
ruthless, indiscriminate massacres and plunderings, what
flower of art could bloom?

The Peace of Westphalia was signed in 1648, but for
the rest of the century there was little sign of recupera-
tion in the province of literature. The universities had
been deserted, the schools closed by hundreds : literary
instincts had to be re-created. The poets had not long
given up writing in Latin, society had not yet given
up talking in French ; and the former still appealed
chiefly to the small public who thought it the highest
excellence in German poetry that it should contain
elegant reminiscences of classical study. The be-
ginnings of a poetry at once popular, secular, and
elevated, were still to seek. The drama, which, largely

owing to the influence of the great Elizabethan stage, had shown marked signs of promise before the war, had now sunk to mere buffoonery, varied to some extent, but not notably elevated, by the importation from Italy of the *Singspiel*, or opera.

The beginning of better things makes its first decided appearance in the writings of the "Swan of Leipzig "— *lege* "goose" notes Carlyle—Gottsched. He devóted himself to the discovery of rules for the practice of literature, and, in particular, to the crying want of the time, the reformation of the German stage. Goose or swan, his achievements in this direction were really valuable. He banished the clown from the boards, and made ordinary theatrical audiences, always largely composed of the common people, take an interest in refined comedy and dignified tragedy. But, as a reformer, he had fatal defects which caused his real services to be overlooked by the stronger spirits who supplanted him. He thought literature should be didactic, had no understanding of its deeper potencies, and judged it by small and pedantic theories. In the drama, whatever did not conform to the rules of Aristotle, as understood or misunderstood on the French stage, was for him barbarous and intolerable. That German literature should have a native character of its own does not appear to have occurred to him, and hundreds of French pieces were translated, adapted, and imitated by him and the large and active school which formed itself about him. When in verse, these are written, like the French, in rhymed alexandrines—a metre which, in a strongly accented language like the

German, has an inexpressibly dreary and mechanical effect.

Over against the school of Gottsched another soon arrayed itself, which bore as its motto the well-known phrase, " Ut pictura, poesis." The theory of this school, whose founders were the Swiss Bodmer and Breitinger, was that poetry should appeal not directly to the understanding or moral sense, but to the fancy. True ; but how may the fancy be best affected ? By pictorial description, was practically their answer—especially descriptions of that which excites the sense of wonder. Poetry was painting in speech, just as painting was poetry in colour and form—it was the essential, not merely the subordinate, excellence of each form of art that it could imitate the effects of the other. And by its success in attaining this aim, not by its observance of any external rules, the merits of any particular production were to be decided. As against Gottsched, the Swiss were clearly right, but the practical result of their teaching was to confuse fatally the limits of the poetic and plastic arts, leading the latter to symbolism, and the former to empty description. However, of the preparatory influences that had yet appeared, theirs was far the most valuable. They did much to introduce a knowledge of English literature into Germany. They rediscovered the Nibelungenlied, and the Nibelungenlied proved that a poem may be truly great without imagery or reflections, simply by the powerful narrative, in the simplest imaginable kind of human speech, of action controlled by passion and character. In their weekly organ (*Discourse der Maler*) they founded a school of genuine, because flexible, tolerant, and sincere criticism ; a school which accustomed the numerous readers whom it influenced to take large views of literature, and to dismiss from their minds the petty arbitrary standards of the " Gottschedianer."

The hour was now come, and with it came *four* men. WIELAND was one of the most versatile of writers, and has many titles to renown, but his principal merit is, perhaps, that in a much deeper sense than Gottsched he assimilated the spirit of French literature, and reproduced in German its purity, lightness, and precision of style. KLOPSTOCK ended the academic imitative manner in German verse, went with virile force and passion to the heart of his subject, and first showed of what heroic tones the language was capable. WINCKELMANN rejuvenated antiquity, and through him the serenity and simplicity of Greek art put an end to the cold ingenuities of the Rococo Renaissance. But none of these men wielded an influence to be compared in width and power and permanence with that of LESSING. By the work which he did in giving national substance and colour to the German drama, he reached the German people as none of his contemporaries could do. But this was only one of the achievements of the many. sided activity of which it is sought in the following pages to give some account. It is enough here to say that wherever his touch was felt, instead of littleness, poverty, and stagnation, it left the stir of life, the energy of large and worthy aspirations. In him Germany may be said to have first become aware of the mighty spiritual destinies towards which the "industrious valour " of the race has since carried her so far.

Gotthold Ephraim Lessing was born on January 22 1729, in the small Saxon town of Kamenz. His family was of Wendish origin, springing originally from one of those small Slavonic communities, relics of pre-Teutonic Germany, which are still found in various parts of Prussia and North Saxony. The "Lessigks" had now, however, been thoroughly Germanized for centuries. They were a solid, respectable, and respected race, filling with credit various civil and ecclesiastical positions, tinctured, too, with learning, and severely Lutheran.

Lessing's father was probably the most learned and the most Lutheran of them all. He studied theology and Church history at the University of Wittenberg, and stood then and thenceforth immovably rooted in the ideas of the Reformation, which he regarded as in all respects a divine event subject neither to criticism nor amendment. It was his earnest wish, and it would have been within his power, to obtain some academic post at Wittenberg; but in 1717 he received from Kamenz, his native town, the offer of a post as catechist and preacher in the Lutheran church there. He obeyed what he considered to be the call of God, and thenceforth his career was confined to the little Saxon town. He became, in course of time, archdeacon, and soon married Justine Salome Feller, daughter of the " Pastor Primarius," or chief Pastor, of Kamenz. On the death of his father-in-law, in 1734, Gottfried Lessing succeeded to his place, and remained there for the rest of his life. He was a devout, laborious, admirable man, saved from any too intolerable narrowness by his true humility and goodness of heart—also perhaps in some degree by his learning. Besides the classics, he knew French and English thoroughly, and had published excellent translations from Superville and Tillotson. His great son honoured and loved him deeply : " How I could praise him, if he were not my father ! " His greatest moral defect was a passionate temper—a fault of which he was pathetically conscious. Lessing once received a mandate from the Duke of Brunswick, forbidding him to defend himself in future against an enemy who had violently and wantonly attacked him, and he tells us that when he felt the hereditary rage seething in his heart, his father's image stood before him. He finds himself biting his underlip in anger, "and at once he stands before me, my father, to the very life. That was a habit of his when anything began to vex him ; and whenever I want to recall his image vividly to my mind, I have only to bite my underlip in the same way. So, too, if anything happens to make me think of him, I may be sure that my teeth will at once fasten on my lip. Good, old lad, good ! I understand thee. So good a man as thou wast ! and thereto so hot tempered a one ! How often hast thou thyself lamented to me— lamented with a manly tear in thine eye—that thou wert so quickly hot, so quick to be carried away by thy heat ! How often hast thou said to me : ' Gotthold, I entreat thee take example by me—be on thy guard ! For I fear— I fear—and I would gladly at least see myself bettered in thee. . . .' There let him stand, biting his passion into silence, a figure not to be regarded without love and admiration."

Lessing's mother was a person of much more common

mould. She reverenced her husband, fulfilled her housewifely duties excellently, and thwarted her children whenever they did anything, which was not seldom, that she did not understand or approve of.

The boy's life at Kamenz was conducted under strict discipline, and in an atmosphere of piety and learning. He was the second surviving child, his sister Dorothea being two years older, and his next brother, Theophilus, nearly four years younger. In his fifth year Gotthold was thoroughly grounded in the Lutheran Catechism. His love of books manifested itself very early, and a painting of him and his brother Theophilus, done when he was six years old, still exists, in which, at his own desire, he was represented with a book on his lap and three great folios at his side.

The father and mother early recognized their son's talent, and meditated great things for him. He should go to the excellent endowed school of St. Afra at Meissen,—one of the three *Fürstenschulen* into which the Elector Maurice of Saxony had transformed three suppressed monasteries; — thence to the university, where, as the scholar of the family, he should prepare himself for the degree of Doctor of Theology;— eventually, if he did not choose to content himself with a pastorate, he might even attain that Professorship of Ecclesiastical History which his father had sorrowfully renounced.

✕ In preparation for these destinies—for St. Afra in the immediate future—Gotthold was sent to the grammar school at Kamenz, which then had the great advantage (if he was in a position to profit by it) of possessing a master of remarkable and stimulating gifts in Johann Heinitz, from Laubau. Heinitz was fond, like Epictetus, of urging on his pupils that the first step towards true knowledge was the casting away of οἴησις — those accepted beliefs which have all the more stiffening power upon the mind because it has never sought for their grounds,— a principle which might plainly be applied, with incalculable results, even to the Pastor's views of the Lutheran Reformation! The schoolmaster, however, vexed the Pastor's soul still more by recommending the study of the drama as a school of eloquence, and even causing his pupils, on one of the yearly *Forstfeste*, to take part in a dramatic representation. Ultimately—but this was after Gotthold had left Kamenz —matters came to such a pass between the old order and the new, the Pastor and the Schoolmaster, that the latter was driven from his post.

The Pastor had succeeded in obtaining a promise from the Elector of a free place at St. Afra for his son, if the latter on reaching his twelfth year could pass the necessary examination. To prepare for this he was sent for a few months to a brother-in-law of his father, an old Fürstenschüler, named Lindner, now a Lutheran clergyman in Putzkau. While under tuition here, Lessing often saw a child of about four years old, whose path he was to cross again—the son of Lindner's friend, Superintendent Klotz, of Bischofswerda. Little Klotz was to grow into a windbag, swollen with pretension and intrigue, and little Lessing was to prick him.

CHAPTER II.

ON June 21, 1741, Gotthold entered St. Afra for
his preliminary examination in Latin, Greek,
Mathematics, and the Lutheran Catechism. He answered excellently, and was placed in the class above
the lowest. And now began five years of study and
discipline arduous even to severity. At half-past four in
summer, and an hour later in winter, every boy rose,
washed himself in the trough in the courtyard, dressed,
cleaned his boots, made his bed, and repaired to the
dining-hall, when the school-day opened with a hymn
and a Latin prayer. This over, the boys might provide
themselves (at their own expense) with a breakfast, which
they obtained from the porter. From 6 to 11, from
1 to 6, and again from 8 to 9.30, were given up to
study or to religious exercises : the monastic spirit still
lingered in the institution (now under the control of
the Oberconsistorium, or Synod of the Lutheran Church
in Saxony), and there was an enormous amount of
church-going. The fare was good enough, in theory,
but the steward who provided it once occasioned,
by persistent ill-fulfilment of his contract, a sort of
insurrection, in which Lessing took a prominent part.

Fires at St. Afra were unknown, intensely cold as is
the winter climate of Central Germany.   There were
about sixty holidays in the year—a string of them
together at Christmas ; no regular vacation, but the boys
might visit their homes for a few days at Whitsuntide.
The great purpose of the school, most of whose hundred-
and-odd pupils were intended for the Church, was to
make good Lutherans and good Latinists.   Greek and
Hebrew were only allotted about seven hours in the week
between them, as against fifteen to Latin.   Mathematics,
physical science, and history came off worse still, and
German received scarcely any direct attention.   But
St. Afra taught thoroughly what it did teach.   Latin was
learned colloquially, as it still is in the German classical
schools, and in the higher classes all instruction was
given in that language.   And there were two peculiar
and admirable features in the St. Afra system : one
hour each evening was devoted to the repetition of
their lessons by the younger boys, the elder ones taking
the place of teachers—an arrangemen' by which the
elders must have benefited immensely ; and every
alternate hour through the school-day was given to
private study—the school programme being then
abandoned, and the pupil allowed to get instruction from
any master in whatever branch of learning his own
inclination led him to pursue.   We have it on record
that Lessing gave these hours mainly to the Latin
dramatists.

The masters of St. Afra were mostly men of some distinction in literature.   The Rector [*Anglice*, Head-master],
Grabner had published an improved and enlarged edition

of Weissenborn's "Introduction to the Arts of Poetry and Oratory in Latin and German," had written poetry himself —or what passed for such in an age when poetry was looked on as an art to be learned—and had thought his own thoughts on philosophic subjects—thoughts which he knew how to communicate in a manner which won the attention of his class. His influence is perceptible in a German essay written by Lessing in the year 1742, on the theme " That one year is like another " (*i.e.* that the world is not growing worse); and also in a later and more remarkable production, a poem (in rhymed alexandrines) on the Plurality of Worlds, in which Lessing attempted to give expression to the new thoughts which had crowded upon him on reading Whiston's "Theory of the Earth," and the " Kosmotheoros " of Huygens. These early productions have no imaginative or descriptive power, but, for one so young, they show a singular acquaintance with philosophic ideas, and an admirable clearness and method.

But the master at St. Afra who exercised the most decided influence on Lessing was Herr Klimm, a mathematician of wide repute. His influence was especially useful in forming a counterpoise to that of the Conrector Höre, whom Lessing regarded as little more than a pedantic grammarian. Klimm, besides being something of a celebrity in his own particular line, was an accomplished classical scholar, and read English, French, and Italian. It was a favourite maxim of his that language is but the instrument of learning, and that a scholar is worth very little without mathematics and philosophy. It is noted of Herr Klimm that he could not preserve order and attention in a large class of average schoolboys, but that certain of the *élite*, among whom was Lessing, were so inspired by him with the passion for learning that they would study with him till midnight—a forbidden thing, certainly, which could only be done in the weeks in which the evening inspection duty fell to him. Under Klimm's guidance Lessing threw himself with great enthusiasm into the study of mathematics. Euclid especially exercised upon him the fascination it has for logical minds, and he translated three or four books from the Greek.

Besides school themes, and the poem already mentioned, there is not much of original production to record during Lessing's St. Afra days. Of most importance was the sketch of a comedy, afterwards worked out at Leipzig, "The Young Scholar," which was intended to ridicule pedantry. He also wrote, at his father's instigation, a tame poem of thanks to Lt.-Col. von Carlowitz, who had given him a scholarship at St. Afra.[1]

We find some "Anacreontic" verses, too, among the productions of his school-days. It was the age of Anacreontics in Germany. Ramler, Gleim, Lange, all the versifiers of the day tried their skill in these elegant and artificial celebrations of the joys of revelry and gallantry.

But if Lessing gave no very decided indications of originality at St. Afra, his progress there was amply sufficient to encourage his father in the high expectations

---

[1] His *Freistelle* from the Elector entailed on the Pastor a payment of about £3 a year, from which the Carlowitz Scholarship released him.

he had formed for him. At first we find him represented in the half-yearly reports as marring, by a certain levity and wilfulness, the impression made by his good looks. His high gifts, we can perceive, were clear from the outset to his masters, but he did not travel smoothly in the beaten tracks which they prescribed. He seems to have shown in these early days a decided, but, in a high-spirited boy, not altogether unwholesome tendency to come into conflict with scholastic law and order. Soon, however, the passion for learning laid firm hold upon him, and thereafter all went well. Good behaviour, an excellent memory, and acuteness of intellect are attributed to him by Höre in 1744. Some eighteen months later Grabner wrote that there was "no region of learning" which his eager intellect did not seek to explore, even to the too great dissipation of his powers. In the following year, 1746, Grabner observes that Lessing is "schooling his spirit"—his disposition, if "too fiery," is yet "anything but perverse," and his progress is great in all his studies. "A good boy, *aber etwas moquant,*" is the comment which we now find appended to his name by one of the official school inspectors.

In 1745 Meissen was entangled in an eddy of the great stream of world-history, and much of the froth and wreckage with which that stream was then bestrewn found its way into St. Afra. Up to this date Saxony had taken no direct part in the second Silesian war. In November, however, Brühl, the Saxon minister, devised, and happily babbled about, his notable plan for descending upon Brandenburg he and Austria in three armies at once; with the result that Brandenburg suddenly, and without babbling, descended upon him. The Prussians invaded Saxony, and on November 29th seized Leipzig. On December 12th, Meissen was occupied for the purpose of securing a passage across the Elbe for Frederick, who was lying at Bautzen. The town had been slightly bombarded on the 9th, and the scholars of St. Afra were gathered for safety into the dining-hall in the basement. The school buildings, however, were untouched, and a few days later Frederick himself, passing through Meissen, assured the Rector, as became a cultured king, that the school should possess all immunities possible in such a time. On the 15th Lessing's countrymen fought their last battle as a nation, with their usual valour and their usual fate, in the half-frozen bogs of Kesselsdorf. The cannonade was heard at St. Afra; and the world of Plautus and Terence, in which Lessing says he then lived, must, for once, one thinks, have seemed very dim and remote to him, as that fateful mutter swelled and sank on the eastern breeze. Studies were, indeed, generally in a disorganized state, nor were things much better even after peace was signed at Christmas.

"You may indeed pity poor Meissen," wrote Lessing to his father, "which now looks more like a charnel-house than the town it was before. Everything is full of stench and filth, and whoever can help coming in keeps as far from it as he can. There are still thirty or forty wounded soldiers lying in most of the houses, whom no one can go very near, for all who are at all dangerously hurt have the fever. It is God's wise providence that this calamity has occurred in winter, for were it summer the pestilence would surely be raging among us. And who can tell what is to happen next?

However, we will trust in God and hope for the best. But there is no place in the town that, in comparison with its former state, looks so pitiable as our school,"—masses of wounded soldiers in it, and numbers of the boys gone home.

Lessing had already found himself longing to enter upon a wider course of study than St. Afra could afford, and was weary of its seclusion and restraint. His petitions to be allowed to leave had been rejected hitherto, but the Pastor had now found means to secure for his son an exhibition at the University of Leipzig, and applied to Grabner for an account of his ripeness. The Rector approved his withdrawal: "He is a horse that must have double fodder. The lessons that are too hard for others are light as air to him. We can hardly do any more with him," and at last the Oberconsistorium, which could have retained him at St. Afra for a year longer, permitted him to go in peace. Lessing delivered the customary farewell speech in Latin, on June 30, 1746, his subject being " The Mathematics of the Barbarian (non-classical) Nations,"—his friend and class-fellow, Birckholtz, replying on behalf of the remaining pupils in a German "poem " on the mathematical attainments of insects.

Lessing left St. Afra in his eighteenth year. A few months previously the great Fürstenschule of Pforta had parted with another pupil, Friedrich Gottlieb Klopstock, who left it at the riper age of twenty-two, after a striking address on the subject of epic poetry, with his mind already fired by the poetic mission he was destined to fulfil. Lessing had no mission. Literature expanded, wide, varied, and all-alluring before him.   But if he had not yet chosen a track, St. Afra had at least thoroughly mapped the land ;—blind paths and pitfalls will have no dangers for him.

CHAPTER III.

LESSING on leaving St. Afra spent three or four
months in the parsonage at Kamenz among six
brothers and sisters, most of whom he could scarcely
have known by sight. In September, 1746, he was
matriculated as student of Theology at Leipzig. The
city was then, as now, but in a much more striking
relative eminence, the great publishing and bookselling
centre of Germany. It was also the centre of the
most powerful literary movement of the day,—that led
by Gottsched,—and the atmosphere of the place was,
as Lessing observes, full of incitements to authorship.
But the young St. Afran soon found, to his no small
perplexity and disgust, that this delightful world
made demands upon him which he was wholly unpre-
pared to meet. Just as at some of the Universities,
such as Jena and Halle, the traditionary tone among
the students was that of the elaborate and cultivated
rowdiness known as Renomisterei, so at Leipzig the
exactly opposite conventions prevailed, and the student
was expected to be "galant."[1]   Here was a quite
unexpected set of problems for Lessing, and the spirit

[1] *Wahrheit und Dichtung.*

of masterful energy with which he dealt with them is very striking. Two years later he described his early life in Leipzig in a sort of "apologia pro vitâ suâ," in which he thus wrote to his mother :—

"I lived for the first months more retired than I had lived even in Meissen. Always among my books, occupied only with myself. . . . I learned to see that books would make me a scholar, but never a man. I ventured forth among my fellows. Good God! what a difference I perceived between myself and them! A boorish shyness, a neglected and awkward body, utter ignorance of the manners of society, a gloomy, unfriendly bearing, in which every one believed he read my contempt for him—these were the good qualities that my self-criticism disclosed. I felt such a shame as I had never felt before. And the effect of it was the fixed determination to better myself in this, cost what it might. I learned to dance, to fence, to vault. . . . I advanced so far in these things, that even those who, by anticipation, had denied me all talent for them, came in some degree to admire me. . . . I sought society, in order that now I might also learn to live. I laid aside grave books for a time, in order to make myself acquainted with others, which are far pleasanter, and perhaps quite as useful."

Among the professors whose lectures he attended, the name of Johann F. Christ deserves special mention. Christ was one of the leaders in the great reformation of scholarship which was then proceeding in Germany— a man who had other conceptions of culture than those of the grammarian, a lover and student of the fine arts, and one of the very first of German *savants* to treat learned subjects in a style which possessed individuality and charm.

Much that is admirable and characteristic in Lessing's writings is traceable to the influence of Christ, who even taught him his peculiar manner of entering upon a subject as it were by a side door—developing his most valuable ideas in the course of a polemical discussion on some apparently trivial circumstance or object.

The great Biblical scholar, Ernesti, too, had his share in developing Lessing's talent, and so had, in a much greater degree, the young and versatile Professor of Mathematics, Kästner, with whom be became personally intimate, and in whose circle he found congenial friends. Gottsched did not attract him in the least; he felt, perhaps, rather than fathomed, his imposing emptiness and fatuity.

But Lessing was not long in coming within the range of an attraction more powerful for him than either society or scholarship. At this time it happened that a certain Frau Neuber, an actress to whom he attributes "a masculine insight," had established herself with an excellent company at Leipzig. The enterprise with which so many minds in Germany were then and afterwards, and, we may add, to such good purpose, concerned,—namely, that of reforming the German theatre and making it an instrument of high popular culture, had a devoted adherent in Frau Neuber. It is true her ideas were those of Gottsched, but the French or imitation-French drama, which she and her company played in Leipzig, was by no means so poor a form of the drama as Lessing's desire to introduce English models afterwards led him to declare. For him, at that time, it was an enchanting revelation. The literature of more than one people had told the young scholar something of the world :—with what delight must he, so informed, and yet so ignorant, have watched, night after night, its passions, heroisms, follies, reflected in living action on the Leipzig stage ! What education could be compared with this ! With special admiration and profit he noted the ideal of manners, never conceived by him before, which Frau Neuber's accomplished actors and actresses exhibited in their polished French comedies. For a time all Leipzig for Lessing was centred on the stage. He soon found a fellow-enthusiast, a shy, awkward, but talented young student named Weisse, who, like him, had tried his hand at a play, and whose passion for the theatre seemed as insatiable as Lessing's. And there was intellect and purpose in their passion. They began to compare, to reflect ; they read English and French plays, and studied all the conditions and possibilities of the drama. The regions behind the scenes, with which they soon made acquaintance, had for them no chilling disillusionment, for they were in search of laws which led them deeper than paint and carpentry and weekly wages. Both of them desperately poor, as it would be reckoned to-day, they gained the glorious privilege of free admission by making translations from the French for Frau Neuber. They used to take part in the consultations of the performers about the rendering of passages and pieces, and Lessing's opinion on these points was soon listened to with much respect. He gained, by his intimacy with the Neuber company, almost as vital a knowledge of the conditions and requirements of the stage as if he had been an actor himself.

Lessing's first acquaintance with the delights of authorship took place under the auspices of a friend whose
slovenly figure will have to shuffle through these pages
for some little time. This was Christlob Mylius, son
(by a second marriage) of a Deacon Mylius, whose
first wife was an elder sister of Lessing's father. His
brother Christlieb had once been tutor to Lessing; and
he had other brothers, Christhold, Christfried, Christhelf,
the name "Christ" entering into all the names of the
Mylius family, as "Gott" mostly did in some form into
those of the Lessings—a circumstance which indicates
the atmosphere of Biblical piety which prevailed in
those regions. Christlob Mylius, however, was not
pious. He had decided talent, but Kamenz was not
proud of him. When the schoolmaster Heinitz was
driven away, Mylius had written a satirical poem, especially severe on Lessing's father, against the civil and
ecclesiastical authorities there, who laid him in prison
the next time he came within their power, and instituted
a prosecution against him. Now he was shuffling in a
painfully un-*galant*, untrimmed, down-at-heel condition
about Leipzig, studying medicine and natural science
with energy and with considerable results, adapting
French dramas for Frau Neuber, now and then coming
out with some shortlived periodical—*The Freethinker*,
Incitements to Pleasantry, *The Investigator of Nature*
—which usually contained a curious mixture of
libertinism, natural science, religion, irreligion, and
other incongruous things. Lessing met Mylius at
Kästner's house, and the two formed a friendship and
literary alliance which lasted a long time. In the

Ermunterungen of Mylius (about the spring of 1747), Lessing first saw himself in print : "Anacreontic" verses which showed a good measure of the dreary cleverness natural to such compositions, and a little drama, "Damon ; or, True Friendship," which is not without vivacity of style. His contributions were much admired, and doubtless he was pressed to join the literary enterprise known as the *Bremer Beiträge*, a journal managed in concert by a number of the most vigorous minds in Leipzig—Adolf Schlegel, the poet Zachariä, Ebert, Mylius (for a short time), and Gellert. But from this circle Lessing held aloof. Since the arrival of Klopstock in Leipzig, the *Bremer Beiträge* had come greatly under his influence, and Lessing, though he fully recognized Klopstock's genius, entertained from the outset a certain repugnance for his "seraphic school" of literature, with its somewhat too emotional and ostentatious earnestness of purpose.

He had not been long in Leipzig before it became clear that the station in life for which he was supposed to be preparing himself was an impossible one for him. He neglected his theological studies, and took up philology instead. After a time even this was abandoned, as far as seeking any regular instruction went. He declared his intention of studying medicine, and began to attend lectures on botany and chemistry. But the theatre occupied him more seriously than anything else : it was thought, and not without reason, that he had even some idea of going on the stage. More than one of the Neuber company had been university students like himself. He soon, indeed, did something which shocked the Kamenz people nearly as much as this would have done. One evening, as the merits of a play of Gottsched's school, which had just been performed, were being discussed, Lessing opposed the general view, and declared it to be bald and dull. " Can *you* make a better, then ? " " I can, and will," said Lessing, and he forthwith set himself to redeem his promise. It has been already mentioned that, while at St. Afra, he had occupied himself with a comedy in which pedantry should be held up to ridicule. An event had lately occurred at Leipzig, which suggested a *dénouement* in which the ridiculous pedant might figure with effect. The Academy of Berlin had offered a prize for a treatise on the Monad Theory of Leibnitz, and one of the candidates—a conceited young Leipzig student, who did not know how much he was ignorant of—had declared publicly that his composition could not fail to win it. His essay had been adjudged to be wholly worthless, and Leipzig had been hugely amused. In Lessing's play, the essay of the young scholar is represented as having been entrusted to a friend to be forwarded to the Academy. In the first scene we see him awaiting with longing the arrival of the post which shall bring the news of his victory. Then he is entangled by his father in an engagement with a wealthy ward of the latter. She loves another, and the play progresses through a variety of comical episodes until the arrival of the Berlin post. He finds his own essay returned to him—the friend announces that, out of regard for his reputation, he did not even send in so unsuitable a composition. The Academy, he writes, did not want to know " What is

3

the grammatical meaning of ' Monas '? Who used it first? What it indicates in Xenocrates? Whether the Monads of Pythagoras are the atoms of Moschus? What do they care for these trivialities, even if there had been anything besides to the real purpose of the theme?" The young pedant is furious, determines to abandon Germany and seek for recognition of his merits elsewhere; and his *fiancée* is left to her lover.

This was Lessing's first important work, and after he had improved it in accordance with suggestions of Professor Kästner (in all Lessing's works he eagerly sought help from any one who had it to give), he brought it to Frau Neuber. She recognized its talent instantly and fully, hailed Lessing as the rising sun of the German stage, and had the play at once put in rehearsal. Her enthusiasm is not very easy to understand at the present day. Certainly the dialogue is vivacious, and the language excellent, in the terse laconic style then admired, but there is only a very superficial attempt at characterization, the incidents show little invention, and oddities of behaviour are insisted upon to monotony. But in Lessing's portrayal of false learning and, by implication, of true, and in his hits at the literary theories of the day, there was a critical intelligence which Leipzig audiences would appreciate; and Frau Neuber knew that they were always particularly delighted with the representation on the stage of any event which could be identified with one that had actually transacted itself in their midst.

Reports of Lessing's doings could not long fail to reach Kamenz, and the inevitable mischief-makers were

soon found to supply them. The facts which reached
the parsonage doubtless did so in a very exaggerated
form; but two of them needed no exaggeration to
convey to the Pastor the blackest view of his son's
courses : he was constantly in the company of that type
of audacious impiety, Mylius, one who feared not God
neither regarded man ; and he was a frequenter of the
theatre, nay, even a daily associate of actors, a class
which even in much more enlightened parts of Germany
than the Lausitz was regarded as hardly within the pale
of salvation. The Pastor's sorrow and indignation found
vent at last in a letter in which, without having heard
Gotthold's side of the question, he thundered to him that
he was going straight to perdition, and summoned him
to immediate repentance and amendment. Lessing was
moved to passionate anger at this hasty and unjust condemnation. He was no profligate—if he had written
verses (some of which had doubtless reached Kamenz)
which represented their author as living for nothing but
kisses and wine, he could, and did, say with Ovid,
" My life is sober, though my Muse be gay." And on
the question of the morality of the stage he was entitled
to form his own opinions. His first impulse on receiving
his father's letter was one of reckless defiance ; he would,
he declared to Weisse, have his name and birthplace
affixed to the playbills of the "Young Scholar," and send
a copy to every dignitary in Kamenz. This reckless
and altogether too Mylius-like proceeding was happily
not carried out; but he left the letter unanswered,
and matters soon came to a dangerous crisis. His
mother had sent him by a friend's hand a Christmas

cake, or "Stollen," such as relatives and friends were and are in the habit of sending to each other at that season. Could she but have foreseen the fate of that cake ! Made by devout hands in the parsonage of Kamenz, it was eaten—so she was correctly informed— in Lessing's rooms in the company of a troop of actors, and a bottle of wine figured at the impious feast.

Rumours of the "Young Scholar" also reached Kamenz, and it was felt that now indeed no time must be lost if Gotthold were to be plucked as a brand from the burning. But what paternal command or entreaty could be expected to weigh with one already so abandoned ? The Lessings saw only one means of gaining their end, and—let us hope with some painful twinges of con- science—the Pastor sent a speedy message to his son: "Set out instantly on receipt of this and come to us. Thy mother is sick to death, and wishes to speak with thee before her end." They little knew the heart on which they played so dangerous a trick. Lessing flung himself at once into a stage coach and started for his long journey in the depth of winter, without having even delayed to provide himself with an overcoat. On the way a period of bitter cold set in, and with it a revulsion of feeling at the parsonage as they thought of the journey they had forced upon him at such a time. Even their previous sorrows, acute as these had been, were now a kind of comfort to them—"He has learned disobedience," thought Frau Lessing ; "perhaps he will not come after all." But when the Leipzig mail arrived, there stood the prodigal indeed, a piteous figure, shivering on the threshold. "How could you come in such weather?"

cried his mother, half-reproachfully. "Dearest mother, did you not wish it?" replied Lessing. "But how glad I am to find that my suspicions were right, and you are well." A smaller and less genial nature might have been deeply injured by the deceit they had practised on him for pious ends, but he let it pass with a large, unconscious generosity. Generous and exalted his mood may well indeed have been just then, and little, perhaps, had he felt the hardship of that winter journey ; for he travelled with the applause still echoing in his ears with which a great capital of culture had welcomed his first play.

CHAPTER IV.

IT was more than a year since Lessing's parents had seen him. He had left them a shy, uncouth, and probably self-important lad, for we are much mistaken if Lessing had not some eye to foibles of his own in the "Young Scholar." They now saw a well-grown, compactly-built youth, showing in his bearing and behaviour the security of the practised athlete and the social culture which he had gained in "Paris-on-the-Pleiss." The head, with its waving light brown hair, was set a little proudly on the strong shoulders; the broad brow and open countenance expressed candour, courage, and genial power. But the look of the large dark-blue eyes, "true tiger eyes," as a later observer described them, must have told that there was "something in him dangerous." His dress in later years was always notably neat and even elegant, and although he was now in need of a new suit, the condition of the attire he wore must have at least made it clear that he was no disciple of the horrible Mylius. In no point, indeed, they soon observed, was he or would he be the blind disciple of any man. His parents might not understand or

approve his ways, but it was evident that he was completely master of himself, knew his mind thoroughly, and
would neither wilfully nor weakly sin against any truth
which he could recognize for such.   Their tone of denunciation was at once abandoned, and day after day the
father and son argued out their differences, if sometimes
with heat, a transient heat, yet at bottom with a cheerful
toleration.   Even the discovery that he had debts was
not found insupportable.   They were paid, with the help
of a benevolent bachelor uncle, but, alas! Lessing's path
in life was never again wholly clear of that dismal swamp.

He stayed till April at Kamenz, and then went back
to Leipzig, to reappear there, with the goodwill of the
family, as Studiosus Medicinæ.   But his true studies
were exactly what they had been before—the theatre
soon occupied him as deeply as ever.   He planned a
tragedy, "Giangir," and partly executed it in rhymeless
alexandrines ; indeed, he and Weisse wrote at this time,
in friendly competition, a number of dramatic fragments,
in some of which their acquaintance with the Restoration
drama of England is clearly visible.   But nothing more
of his came as yet to representation, or even to comple-
tion.   Frau Neuber's theatre was not a commercial
success, and her company was broken up not long after
his return.   What was worse, he had been *bon camarade*
enough to stand security for two or three of the players
in respect of certain loans, and these children of nature
now levanted to Vienna, leaving him to face their creditors
as best he could.   Nor did this trouble his peace of
mind so much as the departure of the beautiful Lorenz,
daughter of an actress of the company.   His relations

with her were never very intimate,[1] but she had fascinated
him for the time, and a letter exists from which it is clear
that he soon afterwards paid a brief visit to Vienna for
the purpose of seeing her again.

Out of the difficulties which now encompassed him
there seemed but one way. In Leipzig he could not
continue to live—he was again deeply in debt there, he
had contracted expensive acquaintanceships, and he had
no means of earning money. He decided to try what
could be done in Berlin. Mylius, who had recently
come into notice through a prize essay for the Academy
of Berlin, had been summoned thither to take part in the
observation of the solar eclipse of July 25, 1748. Mylius
meant to settle there, and saw a prospect of steady occupation, to which desideratum he might, and certainly
would if he were able, help his friend. Lessing determined to follow him to Berlin, seek employment, earn
money, and pay his debts.

This admirable programme was ultimately carried out
in every particular, but for a time it could not even be
begun. Lessing packed up his belongings, including a
good many books which he had gathered about him in
Leipzig, and executed a silent flitting, with no leave-
takings, early in July. On the way he stopped at
Wittenberg, whither he had accompanied a cousin of
his who was travelling to that town through Leipzig.
Here he was destined to remain much longer than he
had expected. He fell ill shortly after he arrived, and
his illness detained him until after the solar eclipse
had taken place. On his recovery he found that

[1] Hempel's "Lessing's Werke," xx. 1, p. 513.

Mylius, disappointed in Berlin, had wandered back
to Leipzig again. Lessing made the best of the
business, was matriculated at Wittenberg, still as student
of medicine, and settled down to spend the winter
there, chiefly in studying classical literature and modern
history. But the drama still occupied him deeply, and
he began or continued several plays—"The Woman-
hater," "Women are Women," and "Justin," among
them. The collection of poems, published some two
years afterwards under the title of "Kleinigkeiten"
(Trifles), now began to be put together for the press.

Lessing disliked his residence in Wittenberg intensely.
His Leipzig creditors persecuted him, and to satisfy them
he would seem to have contracted new obligations in
Wittenberg. At the same time he was earning nothing,
and had no prospect of earning anything. Now again,
however, Berlin seemed to offer him such a prospect.
Mylius had returned thither, and was editing an important journal belonging to the publisher Rüdiger. To
him, some time in November, 1748, Lessing suddenly
fled, leaving behind him, probably as security for his
debts, all his clothing and books.

This bold step meant the abandonment of his
university career, and of the preferments which he
might have hoped to attain at its successful close.
It meant that at twenty years of age, with no definite
expectations of any kind, he would try to make his
living by authorship. It was a perilous enterprise, and
Berlin was a perilous place in which to try it. It is
true that the Prussian capital was becoming, under the
auspices of Frederick the Great and Voltaire, a centre

of science and literature ; but a native-born German had to contend with the neglect of all who were influenced by the court—the Berlin Academy even conducted its transactions in French—and all over Germany literature withered under a system of piratical reprints which there was no law to check. From the theatre there seemed little hope, although he had made proposals to various managers. Life rose like a precipice before him, "black, wintry, dead, unmeasured," and his only hope of getting some foothold on it lay in the horrible Mylius. Mylius, however, was staunch. He introduced his friend to Rüdiger, and in a commission to put in order the publisher's large and excellent library Lessing found at least a ledge to cling to until he saw his way further. He soon began to write occasional reviews in Mylius's paper, translated works from foreign languages for Rüdiger, and worked with the great advantage of having books and learned periodicals at his command.

The parents were naturally much vexed at Gotthold's erratic conduct. They had pardoned much already, not without misgivings, and now they found him abandoning his studies and his stipend, and following his evil genius, Mylius, to a place where he had nothing to depend on save the paltry and uncertain earnings of a literary day-labourer. They required him to return at once to Kamenz, there to render an account of himself, and be despatched, when reduced to a sufficiently submissive frame of mind, to finish his university course at Leipzig—or perhaps the Pastor can get him a modest post through a friend at Göttingen, where he will be at least at a distance from Mylius, and under some kind of supervision.

Lessing's letters of this period will best explain the situation as it appeared to him.

"I could," he writes to his mother on January, 20, 1749, "have long ago got some post here, if I could only have made a better appearance in respect of clothing. . . . Now nearly a year ago you had the kindness to promise me a new suit. You may judge from this if my last request was altogether too unreasonable. But you refuse it me, under the pretext that I am here in Berlin for the satisfaction of some other person. I will not doubt that my *Stipendien* [exhibition, partly defrayed by Kamenz, to permit him to study at the university] will go on at least till Easter. I think, therefore, that my debts will be fairly covered with them. But I see well that your injurious opinion of a person [Mylius] who, if he never did me services before, certainly does so now, just as I need them most —that, I say, this injurious opinion is the chief reason why you are so opposed to my undertakings. It seems as if you held him for an abomination of all the world. Does not this hatred go too far? It is my comfort that I find a number of upright and distinguished folk in Berlin who make as much of him as I do. But you shall see that I am not tied to him."

He will leave Berlin if they positively require it, but he will not go home, nor, for the present, to any university. He will try his fortune in Vienna, Hamburg, or Hanover, and learn at least to fit himself to the facts of life. Whatever happens, he will write to his parents and "never forget the benefits I have received from you." Again on April 10, 1749, he writes:

"I have been some days in Frankfurt [on a theatrical enterprise?] and that is the reason why I received your letter with enclosure of nine thalers somewhat late and am only now able to answer it.

"You insist upon my returning home. You fear that I might go to Vienna with the intention of becoming a writer of comedies there. You are sure that here I am doing hackwork for Herr

M [ylius] and enduring hunger and care thereby. You even write
to me quite plainly that what I wrote to you of various opportunities
I had of settling here was all pure falsehood.   I beg of you
most earnestly to put yourself an instant in my place, and consider
how one must be pained at such ungrounded reproaches, whose
falseness, if you only knew me a little, must be palpably clear to
you. Yet, more than at anything else, I must wonder that you have
served up again this old reproach about my comedies.   I never
told you I would give up writing for the theatre. . . . I only
wish that I had written comedies incessantly . . . those of mine
which have reached Vienna and Hanover have been very well
paid for [adaptations from the French, probably, with a play, " The
Old Maid," evidently inspired by the pinch of hunger and little
else.   There is now a dawn of hope in this quarter, but he paints
in brighter colours than it had]. . . .   As concerns the post at
Göttingen, I pray you to do your very utmost about it, but until
it is sure, I will not come home, and have spent your nine thalers
on a new suit. . . . I want nothing now but my linen and my books,
which you may be able to redeem for me from Wittenberg, and
send here." [1]

And on the 28th of April :

"I have just this moment received your letter of 25 April,
which I answer at once, the more gladly as it was the more pleasing
to me. . . . I am longing for the arrival of my box, and again
entreat you to put in all the books I have named to you in one of
my letters.   I would ask also for the chief of my MSS., including
the sheets entitled 'Wine and Love.'   They are free imitations of
Anacreon [rather, of Anacreon's imitators] of which I made some in
Meissen.   I do not think the strictest moralist can lay them heavily
on my soul :—
              'Vita verecunda est, Musa jocosa mihi.'
So did Martial [*recte* Ovid] excuse himself in a similar case.   And
one must know me little who thinks that my feelings are in the
least harmony with them. . . .   In truth the cause of their existence
is merely my desire to try my strength in all varieties of poetry. . . .

---

[1] The correspondence is in parts epitomized.

If I could rightly claim the title of a German Molière as you scornfully dub me, I should be assured of an immortal name. Truth to say, I would indeed most gladly deserve it. . . . I cannot understand why a writer of comedies cannot be a good Christian. A writer of comedies is a man who paints vices from their ridiculous side. Must a Christian, then, not laugh at vice? Does vice deserve so much respect as that? And how if I even now promised to make a comedy which theologians should not only read but praise? Do you think that impossible? How if I wrote one on the freethinkers, and those who despise your cloth? "

On May 30, 1749, he writes to his father :

"I have duly received the boxes with the specified contents. I thank you for this great proof of your kindness, and would be more profuse in my thanks if, in short, you did not still so utterly mistrust me, and get me into very ill repute by the kind of inquiries you make from all sorts of people who have no concern with my affairs. Shall I call my conscience—shall I call God to witness? I should be less accustomed than I am to regulate my actions according to my moral sense if I could err so far. But time shall judge. Time shall teach you whether I have reverence for my parents, conviction in my religion, and morality in my daily life. Time shall teach whether he is the best Christian who has the principles of Christianity in his memory and, often without under-standing them, in his mouth, goes to church and observes all the customs as everybody else does, because they are usual ; or he who has once rationally doubted, and has reached conviction by the way of investigation, or at least is still endeavouring to reach it. The Christian religion is not a thing that a man should accept on the mere word of his parents. Most people, indeed, inherit it from them as they do their property, but they show by their behaviour what kind of Christians they are. So long as I do not see one of the chiefest commands of Christianity, *to love our enemies*, better observed, so long shall I doubt whether those are really Christians who give themselves out for such."

In this letter Lessing veils in Latin from the maternal

eye an injunction to his father not to let his view of Mylius be coloured by feminine prejudices.

Little by little he made his way. Small employments of various kinds in the literary line came in; he made important acquaintances, personally and by correspondence; his publications attracted attention. Among these were "The Old Maid," and a really interesting letter in rhymed alexandrines to Herr Maspurg, editor of a musical journal, on the rules of the "gay sciences" (Wissenschaften zum Vergnügen), particularly referring to music and poetry. In 1750 he started, in concert with Mylius, a journal entitled "Contributions to the History and Improvement of the Theatre," whose title may best explain its contents. The second issue contained a translation by Lessing of the "Captivi" of Plautus, and the third an admirable criticism of the same play. The enterprise came to a sudden end with the appearance of the fourth number. Mylius had asserted in it that the Italian stage had never produced a good play, and Lessing refused to give any further support to a theatrical journal which could betray such gross ignorance in its own special province.

From Berlin he again wrote to his father on November 2, 1750:

". . . You do me wrong if you think that I have already again changed my mind about Göttingen. I assure you again that I would go there to-morrow were it possible. Not because things are going particularly badly with me in Berlin just now, but because I have given you my promise. . . . The continuance of the journal you know of [*Theatrical Contributions*, not continued after all] and the translation [for Rüdiger] of Rollin's 'Roman History' are taking up more of my time than I like. Since

I purpose, moreover, bringing out at Easter a volume of my theatrical works, already long promised in the literary journals of Jena,[1] likewise a translation from the Spanish of the 'Novellas Exemplares' of Cervantes, I shall not have to complain of *ennui.* . . . I have for some time spent much diligence on the Spanish lauguage, and think I shall not have my labour in vain. As it is a language not over well known in Germany, I think it should in time be useful to me. . . .

"The younger Mylius has fallen out with the elder Rüdiger, and writes no more for his newspaper. They have more than once tried to get me to take his place, if I cared to lose my time with these political trivialities [political journalism then not daring to be anything else than trivial]. . . .

"Whoever wrote to you that I am very badly off, because I no longer have my board and other remuneration from Herr Rüdiger, has told you a great lie [Lessing has little reason to feel kindly towards those who ply his father with information about his doings]. I have never wished to have anything further to do with this old man as soon as I had made myself thoroughly acquainted with his large library. This is done, and therewith we have parted. My board in Berlin is the least of my cares. I can get an excellent meal for," say, 1½d.

"De la Mettrie, of whom I have sometimes written to you, is physician to the king here. His book, 'L'homme Machine,' has made a great stir. Edelmann is a saint compared to him. I have read a work by him, called 'Anti Sénèque ou le souverain bien,' which has gone through twelve editions. You may judge of its abominable character by the fact that the king himself [even he !] threw ten copies of it into the fire."

There was some reason in the Pastor's dislike of Berlin as a place of residence for a talented lad of

---

[1] One Naumann, a friend of Lessing and editor in Jena, announced, on October 18, 1749, that the "ingenious Herr Lessing" would shortly publish the following plays :—" The Young Scholar," "The Old Maid," "Strength of Imagination" ["The Woman-hater "?], "Women are Women," "The Jew," "The Freethinker."

twenty.   Lessing himself published, in 1749, a tale in
verse called "The Hermit," which was a fairly good
imitation of a thing better left unimitated, the " Contes "
of Lafontaine.

Among the eminent men whom he at this period came
into contact with, Voltaire stands conspicuous.   He had
employed Lessing to translate into German certain
pleadings of his in that lawsuit with the Jew Hirsch out
of which he came with such discredit, and Lessing often
dined at his table while these proceedings were in progress.   That a writer so fastidious as Voltaire should
have engaged Lessing to translate him speaks strongly
for the reputation which the latter had even then gained
as a master of German prose.

CHAPTER V.

THE volume of theatrical works spoken of in the Jena journal was to contain six plays. Of these, however, only one, "The Old Maid," reached publication at present, and "Women are Women," an adaptation from Plautus, was never finished. The "Freethinker" reminds us of Lessing's defence of comedy, on the ground that it might be used to ridicule those who despise religion. But Adrast, the freethinker, is not a ridiculous figure—he is highly virtuous in character, his faults are those of the head, and he is ultimately brought to see his errors by the spirit of self-sacrifice and benevolence exhibited by his Christian friends. "The Jews" is perhaps the most interesting of all these plays, considered as a revelation of Lessing's mind ; and indeed none of them has much other interest for readers of to-day. The lot of the Jews in Germany was then, and for long afterwards, a very grievous one. In Prussia their condition was better than elsewhere, but even there, and under a monarch who had begun his reign with a proclamation of universal toleration, they had much injustice to endure. They had to pay toll on their own bodies like merchandize at the gates of Berlin, and a heavy

4

fine had to be paid on the marriage of every Jew, which Frederick, cynically business-like as usual, exacted in the form of a compulsory purchase from his new china factory. And, of course, the indirect results of these insulting penalties and restrictions were far more grievous than the direct ones. Jewish children could not walk in the streets of Berlin without being stoned and hooted—for which reason even Mendelssohn, a man whose genius has helped to make the city where he lived illustrious, was obliged, as he himself tells us, to imprison his little ones all day long in a silk factory.

Lessing's drama champions the oppressed race in its representation of a noble Jew who renders a perilous service to a Christian. It was the first stroke in that combat with tyrannical prejudices which so deeply marks the character of his influence in every sphere in which it operated.

In the comedies produced at this time the influence of the French stage, and especially of Molière, is decidedly predominant. But in the tragic fragment named " Henzi," which was written in 1749, we perceive the effects of a German translation of Shakspere's "Julius Cæsar," which was published by Count von Borgk in 1741, and which is reckoned one of the landmarks of German literature. Three "republican tragedies" were planned by Lessing under its inspiration—"Virginia" (afterwards developed into "Emilia Galotti"), "Brutus" (of the Tarquinian days), and "Henzi." The subject of the last-named play was offered him by contemporary history in Switzerland. The Republic of Berne had long been a prey to gross misgovernment on the part of a small number of families who had possessed themselves of the resources and offices of the State, misusing their unlawful power as shamefully as any dynastic sovereign had ever done. Remonstrance having been tried in vain, a conspiracy was formed among the citizens in 1749 for the purpose of restoring, if necessary by force, the equal laws of the Republic. In this conspiracy a leading part was taken by Samuel Henzi, a man who appears to have been a very Brutus in nobility and purity of character, and whose extraordinary intellectual gifts had gained him a European reputation in the world of letters. The conspiracy was discovered in time to allow of the arrest of the ringleaders on the day appointed for the outbreak of the revolt, and Henzi, with two others, were put to death, after torture had been vainly used in the hope of extorting further revelations.

Lessing's fragment, amounting to some six hundred lines, was first published in 1753, when its importance was warmly recognized by the great Göttingen scholar and critic Michaelis. By the enthusiasm for high human qualities which pervades it, and the absence of any love-story from the plot, it shows the share which " Julius Cæsar " had in its production. Lessing had declared, in the first number of the *Theatrical Contributions*, that "if in dramatic poetry the German will follow his natural impulses, our stage will rather resemble the English than the French." But the French unities were intended to be observed, as indeed they are more or less strictly in all Lessing's plays, and he still finds the rhymed alexandrine the proper vehicle for the tragic drama :—

> " The love I bear thee, friend,
>   Were it not strangely shown
> Did I augment thy griefs
>   By telling of my own ? "

This is the practical effect of the metre in German, and one cannot regret that he never completed his attempt to force a great tragic theme into such a vesture.

Lessing, as we have seen, declined the editorship of Rüdiger's journal when that office was vacated by Mylius. But on the death of Rüdiger, in 1751, he accepted from the new proprietor, Rüdiger's son-in-law, Voss,[1] the management of a literary supplement, appearing every month under the title of " The Latest from the Realm of Wit." Here, and in reviews contributed to the journal for the next five years, Lessing began to show clearly what a powerful and original critical force had entered Germany in him. From the beginning he took his stand outside all the petty literary cliques which among them absorbed almost all the literary activity of the day, and were the bane of healthy criticism. He scoffed at Gottsched and his pettifogging " Art of Poetry." He says of a work of Bodmer's that if, as had been proposed, books intended to be read beyond Germany should be printed in Roman letters, " Jacob and Joseph " might safely be left in Gothic. He added his voice to the acclamations which greeted Klopstock's " Messiah," and pointed with bitterness to the fact that it was reserved for a foreign prince (the King of Denmark) to enable the

---

[1] From whom the paper took, and still bears, the title of the *Vossische Zeitung.*

great German national poet to devote himself wholly to his mission. But Klopstock's strained and too emotional diction, and still more that of his shallow imitators, was ridiculed unsparingly. He utterly refused to bend to the dictatorship which Paris then exercised over Berlin in literary matters, and denounced the licentiousness of tone which, he declared, had stained the reputation of every French writer from the great Corneille down to Piron.

Lessing's criticisms in the *Vossische Zeitung* won him, as they deserved to do, much attention. Young as he was, he spoke with learning, consistency, and good sense. His vivid style, which was beginning to show his later mastery of metaphor and satire, and, still more, his unmistakable passion for truth, for seeing things simply as they are, carried his ideas home to their mark, and he began, with these criticisms, to be a serious power in German literature.

Towards the end of 1751, however, he felt that he had been producing too rapidly and absorbing too little— that he needed a season of retirement, especially from journalistic work ; and he determined to withdraw to Wittenberg, where his brother Theophilus was then a student at the university, and there take out his long-postponed degree of Magister. Before his departure, however, he was destined to be involved in an unfortunate quarrel with Voltaire, which had serious consequences for him in later life. Voltaire's secretary, Richier de Louvain, had lent Lessing a set of proofs of his master's forthcoming " Siècle de Louis XIV." It was a work eagerly looked for by all Europe, and Voltaire intended to gratify Frederick by letting him have the earliest possible copy of it. Lessing was to have returned the proofs in three days, but carelessly lent them to a German friend, in whose house they were seen by a lady intimately acquainted with their author. She, who had begged in vain for a sight of the precious sheets, instantly taxed Voltaire with perfidy in the excuses he had made for his refusal. Voltaire turned furiously on his secretary, the latter flew to Lessing; but Lessing, meantime, utterly ignorant of the tumult he had caused, had repossessed himself of the proofs and taken them with him to Wittenberg. The work had deeply fascinated him, and he had still a few sheets to read. Voltaire's state of cold rage on making this discovery may be realized with the help of the letters which he now wrote to the " Candidat en Médecine " at Wittenberg, entreating the return of his proof-sheets, and adding various excellent reasons why a young man, at the beginning of his career, should not carry out Lessing's presumable intention of issuing a stolen edition or translation of the work —a course to which even M. Lessing's distinguished capacities could not reconcile either its author or its publisher. Lessing of course returned the proofs without delay, but he accompanied them with an epistle in Latin which, he observed, M. Voltaire was not likely to publish if he ever gave an account of the matter; and he judged rightly, for it has vanished. This affair made a great stir in Berlin at the time, and must have been reported, with what colouring we may imagine, to Frederick himself; who will remember it the next time he hears the name of Lessing.

CHAPTER VI

L ESSING'S second residence in Wittenberg, where he lodged with his brother Theophilus, began at the end of December, 1751. For one year he lived a quiet and studious life here. Among classical authors we find that Martial and other epigrammatists were now closely studied. And as the study of the laws of any form of literary art invariably impelled Lessing to test his theories by experiment, he wrote a number of epigrams, and attained such facility in their composition that an unpremeditated "Sinngedicht" would fall from his lips whenever he heard of anything that suggested one— a circumstance also recorded of his Leipzig friend Kästner.

The Wittenberg Library was very rich in works connected with the history of the Reformation, and Lessing now studied this subject with great zeal, and made various projects in connection with it.

On April 29th he took his degree of Magister Artium, after the usual public disputation, on what subject we know not.

He had, in March, made an important acquaintance. Gottlob Samuel Nicolai, brother of the more famous

Nicolai, the " Proctophilosoph " of " Faust," at whom Goethe and his circle aimed so many bitter shafts, passed through Wittenberg and sought out Lessing. The two young scholars—for Nicolai, though a professor of philosophy at Halle, was only twenty-four— became warm friends, and Lessing wrote him a rather sentimental farewell ode on his departure.

In May Lessing and Theophilus were deep in the study of a new poetical translation of Horace, which had just been published by Herr Pastor Lange, of Laublingen, a member of the Berlin Academy. Pastor Lange had already acquired some fame as a lyrist—his translation of Horace was paraded as the result of nine years of diligent toil, it was lauded to the skies by his literary friends, it was dedicated to Frederick the Great, and the author had received a congratulatory letter from the king's own hand. In short, Pastor Lange had grown to be a windbag of most imposing dimensions, and the times were then getting dangerous for windbags. Lessing and his brother went through the translation, comparing it carefully with the original, and found no less than two hundred " childish blunders." A " Don Quixote of learning," as Lessing once, with great aptness, named himself, could not keep his sword in its sheath on such an occasion of quarrel as this, and, after throwing off a brief and trenchant criticism of Lange, he wrote to Nicolai, telling him what a shrewd thrust this windbag was likely to receive. But Nicolai, an intimate friend of Lange's, was quite opposed to any Quixotic procedures—a very powerful giant this, he answers in effect—has great influence at court (Frederick's court), and will never forgive a public exposure ; there are better ways of dealing with him than the Quixotic—put up your sword, and see if, instead of running him through, you cannot merely bleed him a little—send him your annotations, and make him pay you handsomely for a private lesson in Latin. With Lessing's consent, Nicolai would approach Lange with this proposal.

As Lessing's answer has been variously explained by his biographers, it may be well to give its text :—

" . . . I am satisfied also with your proposal concerning the criticism on Herr Lange's translation of Horace. I will, if you think well of it, write to him as soon as possible, and send him, with all politeness, just a hundred grammatical blunders to begin with. I shall see how he takes it, and act accordingly. . . . "

Writing eighteen months afterwards, Lessing positively asserted that no thought of accepting Nicolai's proposal, so far as it involved any demand for payment, had ever entered his head. Probably he did not wish to offend his new friend by letting him see that he thought the proposal one of very dubious propriety. And it is certainly clear that he gave no authority to Nicolai to act as intermediary between himself and Lange, declaring, on the contrary, that he would communicate with Lange direct. He never did so, and for the present, as far as Lessing was concerned, the matter rested there ; where it would have been much better if the officious Nicolai had let it rest.

Another work which now went near to receiving serious damage at Lessing's hands was the "Dictionary of Universal Literature," edited by Professor Jöcher, of Leipzig, and concluded this year. Jöcher, who was no pretender like Lange, but only an unmethodical, in-

accurate, sleepy kind of professor, received the attack
of his young critic (private, in the first instance) with
a simple humility and dignity which at once appeased
Lessing's altogether too tigerish fury; and his strictures
and corrections were ultimately printed as a supplement
to the " Dictionary."

As we have mentioned, the Library of Wittenberg was
very rich in Reformation literature. Lessing loved the
atmosphere of a library, and spent many hours of pleasant
exploration there.   Among the fruit which these hours
bore was a study of an episode in the life of Luther, which
the idolaters of the Reformer, nowhere so narrow and
prejudiced as at Wittenberg, had grossly misrepresented
to the discredit of a certain enemy of Luther's named
Simon Lemnius.   Lemnius had admittedly opposed and
scurrilously slandered Luther.   Lessing shows that he
did so only after Luther had set on foot a vindictive
persecution against him which ultimately drove him out
of Wittenberg ; and that the only motive for this persecution was that Lemnius had written in praise of the
learning and ability of the Prince-Archbishop, Albrecht of
Mainz.   Nothing was more hateful to Lessing than such
intolerance, and he spoke his mind about it fully and
fearlessly.   He wrote with deep admiration of Luther's
general character, but, as he has more than once remarked, it is against those whom he most warmly
admires that an honest critic must stand most vigilantly
on his guard.

The "Rettung," or Vindication of Lemnius, was
published in a series of letters to an imaginary friend,
which appeared in the following year.   It was the first

of those " Vindications " which form so fine and characteristic a feature of Lessing's literary work.

Towards the end of the year 1752 he decided that
he had had enough of Wittenberg, and prepared to
return to Berlin. We may fix this date as the first great
turning-point in his literary life. Much of what he had
done hitherto was slight and hurried—all of it had the
nature rather of training and exercise than of serious
performance. The year at Wittenberg was one of
leisurely study and leisurely production, unaffected by
the stress of journalistic necessities. In it his powers
ripened with quick and kindly growth ; he began to
discover, as every great writer must spend some time in
doing, the style in which he could express himself with
strength and freedom ; and from henceforth he may take
the rank, really as well as formally, of Master of the
liberal Arts.

CHAPTER VII

L ESSING now took up his quarters in the neigh-
bourhood of the office of his employer, Voss, and
dwelt there with much content and profit to himself for
about three years. He resumed his work on the *Vossische Zeitung*, and Voss, like Rüdiger, gave him much
to do in the way of translations of foreign works, some
of which he enriched by introductions from his own
hand.

The horrible Mylius is now about to depart from the
scene which, unless we judge him purely from the
Kamenz standpoint, he has not altogether disgraced.
He received, in February, 1753, a commission from a
body of persons interested in science (among them the
King of Denmark) to go on a voyage to Surinam and
the Danish Antilles, there make observations in natural
history, and, generally, collect all the information he could
bearing on science, industry, and art. He was promised,
on his return, a professorship at Göttingen. It is clear
that the Kamenz view of Mylius did not prevail everywhere, but it is clear also that there was too much justi-
fication for it. Mylius left Berlin in February, with a

hearty God-speed from Lessing in the *Vossische Zeitung;* but six months afterwards had only got as far as Holland on the way to Surinam, having spent the intervening time in wandering about Germany on a desultory sort of Epicurean journey. Next he proceeded to London, where, as Lessing tried to urge in his favour, he studied various collections and institutions, with which it would serve him to be acquainted. But the money which should have taken him to the Antilles was now run out, his health had run out with it, and in March, 1754, there was an end of his wasted life.

Lessing mourned deeply for his first and faithful friend, and did what he could for his memory ; but by this time he had formed many new and worthier friendships in Berlin. He had made the acquaintance of Prémontval, the eminent mathematician and philosopher, whom the Jesuits had driven from Paris, and with whom he could carry on that vehement argumentative satirical talk in which he loved to develop and test his ideas. Gumperz, a Jew of high scientific attainments, who was zealous for the diffusion of culture among his countrymen, must also be mentioned, were it only for the fact that through him Lessing became acquainted with Moses Mendelssohn, then a clerk in the silk factory of one Bernard. The little Jew, with his deformed person, stammering tongue, and clear blue eyes, through which looked one of the gentlest, bravest, wisest souls in Germany, was first introduced to Lessing as a worthy antagonist in chess. They soon found a deeper bond of union, and became inseparable. In the following year, 1755, Lessing met Nicolai, the "Proctophilosoph," whose acquaintance with

himself and Mendelssohn had very important literary results.

In the summer of 1753 he published two duodecimo volumes, entitled, "Writings of G. E. Lessing," introduced by a preface which was written in a tone of sincere modesty. In the first volume, which contained poetry alone, we have some three hundred pages of odes, epigrams, and songs, with twenty-three Fables— decidedly the biggest and most varied sheaf that Lessing had yet bound together. One cannot but examine with deep interest the characteristics of such a volume, produced by such a mind as Lessing's, at a time when Herder had lived nine years and Goethe four ; when Thomson, Gray, and Collins were preparing English taste for Scott, Coleridge, and Wordsworth ; when Rousseau's yearnings to recall old Saturn's blameless reign were urging men to seek for lost Nature in the wreck of civilization ; when the misty grandeurs and vast oceanic passions of Celtic Ossian were about to touch some of the deepest sympathies of the age. In what relation does this volume of Lessing's poetry stand to that great awakening and expansion of the human spirit which manifested itself in England and Germany in the form of a literary renascence, and in France as a tremendous political convulsion?

Of the literary movement Lessing has been called one of the chief precursors. Let us consider briefly what were the chief characteristics of that movement, and ask ourselves how far his lyrical poetry can be said to have shared them.

In the first place we note that its ideas are often

obscure, and this is a great part of the secret of its power. Men were tired of living in the narrow, well-explored world of logically verifiable truth. The new literature was one of experiment and adventure—it opened out vast horizons on every side—its meanings were often impalpable as perfume—it made men feel without always troubling itself to make them understand. Nowhere, perhaps, has this characteristic of the modern spirit been better expressed than by Walt Whitman, himself a great representative of that spirit, in his poem on the patient spider :—

" A noiseless, patient spider,
 I mark'd where on a little promontory it stood isolated,
 Mark'd how, to explore the vacant vast surrounding,
 It launch'd forth filament, filament, filament out of itself,
 Ever unreeling them, ever tirelessly speeding them.

 And you, O my soul, where you stand,
 Surrounded, detached, in measureless oceans of space,
 Ceaselessly musing, venturing, throwing, seeking the spheres to
   connect them,
 Till the bridge you will need be formed, till the ductile anchor
   hold,
 Till the gossamer thread you fling catch somewhere, O my
   soul ! "

With its love of the undefinable is connected the wonderful rhythmical beauty of the new poetry. In the rich, luxurious, delicate music of Goethe, in the passionate quiver of Heine's lines, in the virile march of Schiller, the golden strength and fulness of Keats, the piercing sweetness of Coleridge, the spiritual melodies, full of surprise and enchantment, of Shelley, was sought to be expressed that which eluded words.

But most striking of all the features of the modern renascence of literature is its passion for external nature. In nothing was it so original as in this—by nothing else has it so profoundly affected the spiritual lives of men.

Now as regards these three traits of modern poetry, Lessing's poems do not give the least hint of what time was so soon to bring forth. He is never indefinite —one never feels in reading him that he is trying to indicate, to suggest, an idea too vast or subtle for utterance. Nor has he a note of music in him; his metre is correct and solid, but in spite of his felicity of expression (always greater, however, in prose than in verse) it is as unlike music as walking is unlike flying. And as for Nature, in the sense of woods, mountains, seas, and the like, its beauty and significance simply did not exist for him. His friend Kleist, the " Poet of the Spring," was fond of communing with Nature. "When you go to the fields," said Lessing, " I go to the coffee-house." The titles of the "Songs " in this volume tell their own tale—"The Drunken Poet's Praise of Wine," " Phyllis to Damon," " Phyllis Praises Wine," " The Philosophic Drinker," "The Kisses," " Laziness." Here is the dismally vivacious "Anacreontic" vein in full force. But is this all ? Let us see what Lessing has to say about "The Rain." Here it is :—

> " It rains and rains, and will not stop,
> So plains the peasant for his crop.
> But what care I for wet or fine,
> So be it rain not in my wine?"

Besides these "songs" we find here a few odes on various subjects, which are chiefly interesting for the reverence they display for the character of Frederick the Great, who is constantly alluded to.

The most interesting part of the volume is that which contains the Fables and Epigrams—two forms of composition which Lessing had not previously attempted. The Fable he had long studied—Phædrus had been one of his most cherished authors, and he was occupied with the subject up to his last days. Here, indeed, as in his taste for "Anacreontic" poetry, he was only following a fashion of the time—a fashion of which Goethe, who held that the decline of poetry among the Persians was due to the introduction, from Hindostan, of the Fables of Pilpay and the game of chess, has traced the origin in a passage full of mingled pity and satire. It was decided, Goethe observes, by the critical authorities of the time, that poetry must be didactic—it should convey a definite moral lesson. It was also decided that it should present the reader with incidents or descriptions which would excite his sense of wonder. The kind of composition, then, which contained most of the didactic and most of the wonderful must plainly be the highest; and nothing could be at once more wonderful and more didactic than the Fable.

Lessing's essays in this line spring, as production with him so very often did, from a critical investigation into the theory of the subject. His discussions on the nature and history of the Fable, which were published as a preface to a large collection of his fables in 1759, contain the most interesting criticisms of contemporary

opinion on the subject.   He defines the Fable as a tale
which shall describe an action that illustrates a moral
truth, and, in contradistinction to the drama or epos,
shall cease the instant the didactic end is gained. As for
the sense of wonder, to excite which some had absurdly
supposed the talking animals to be introduced, Lessing
shows that it is no part of the fabulist's aim to excite
this feeling, the talking animals being fully accounted
for by the fact that the characters of the various species
are so firmly defined in the popular imagination.

Lessing's own fables are as clear, pithy, and laconic,
and as distinct from the more ornate and literary fables
of Gellert, as his theory demanded.   But about the best
work, even of his own school, as, for example, in Esop,
there is often a certain suggestion of humour and of
picturesqueness, which is rarely to be observed in
Lessing's.   One of his best is that of the carven bow :—

"A man had an excellent bow of ebony, with which he shot
very far and very true, and which he prized exceedingly.   Once,
however, as he looked at it attentively, he said : 'After all, you
are not quite fine enough.   Your smoothness is your only ornament.
It is a pity !   But we can settle that,' he thought, ' I will go and
get the best artist I can to carve figures on the bow.'   He went,
and the artist carved a whole hunting scene on the bow ; and what
could have better suited the bow than a hunting scene ?

"The man was delighted. 'Dear bow, you deserve your
decorations !'   Then he goes to try the bow ; he bends it, and—it
breaks."

This fable, as Mr. James Sime observes, is an excellent illustration of the great principle that governed
all Lessing's criticism—that each form of art attains its

true perfection only in developing its own special capacities.

As with the Fable, so Lessing's study of the Epigram produced first a number of epigrams, and afterwards a critical essay on the subject. The latter, which was not published till 1771, is certainly one of the most brilliant and thoughtful of his prose works. The true nature of the Epigram he deduced from its original intention. He considered that it sprang from the monumental inscription; and when severed from the stone and taken into literature, he held that it must produce the same total effect as that which had been produced by the monument and the inscription together. The monument, visible at a distance, awakens curiosity: we approach, and the inscription gives the desired explanation. An epigram should effect the same alternation of feeling— first, expectation or curiosity, then the satisfaction of disclosure. From the connection with the monument, Lessing is also able to deduce a number of valuable conclusions as to the kind of subject with which an epigram should deal, the nature of its style, and so forth.

The monumental theory of the origin of the literary Epigram, however probable it may be, has no historical evidence of any kind to support it. At the same time it is an admirable "working hypothesis," and introduced light and order into a subject which sadly wanted them —excellent authorities having even defined an epigram to be "any short poem." Lessing's own epigrams, however, are often commonplace and often coarse. Those on Voltaire's death, on Bodmer's poem "The Deluge," the monostich on a hanged criminal, "He rests in peace, when winds are still," and a few others, have excellent point and wit. But of the majority of these poems—lyrics, epigrams, odes, and what not—one can hardly think that many would care to look into them now, were Lessing not the king of modern critics and the author of the three noble dramas which endowed German literature with a classical style.

The first volume of the " Writings " was speedily followed by a second, containing twenty-five Letters on various literary subjects—a form of composition which, like the dialogue, like every form to which he could impart dramatic movement, suited Lessing's genius admirably. These Letters contain the fragment of " Henzi," already mentioned; also the Vindication of Lemnius; a discussion on Klopstock's Messias, with a translation of part of it into Latin hexameters; and some criticism of Jöcher's Dictionary.

One of them involved Lessing in that public controversy with Lange which Nicolai had been so anxious to prevent. Lessing, in his twenty-fourth Letter, points out fourteen gross blunders as examples of the multitude which, to his amazement, he had found on examining the much-lauded translation of Horace. Lange instantly attacked his critic with great violence in a letter to the *Hamburg Correspondent*, a paper which had reviewed Lessing's Letters. Out of the fourteen blunders adduced by Lessing, Lange set aside four as mis-prints, admitted only two as genuine mistakes, and sneered at the character of Lessing's scholarship, which, he said, would fit him better for a proof-reader in a printing-office than for a critic of philology. All this amounted to very little,

for Lange was evidently no match for Lessing, either in
taste or scholarship; but he attacked Lessing's honour
too, and, to the astonishment of the latter, roundly
accused him of demanding, as the price of the sup-
pression of this very criticism, a sum equal to that
which a publisher would have paid him for its publication — a proposal which Lange indignantly rejected.
Unhappy windbag, which could not decently subside
at the first prick ! Lessing's criticism had been—
not exactly polite, for he was never polite to preten-
tious incapacity, but at any rate not unpardonably un-
civil. Now, however, he flew at Lange like a wolf.
His " *Vade Mecum* for Herr Lange" ("Vade
Mecum," because Lange had used the term as a
sneer at Lessing's duodecimo volume of "Schriften "),
reasserted with unanswerable force the original criticisms,
and left Lange's reputation as a scholar irreparably
damaged, by convicting him of at least one serious
mistake in every ode of the first book. As to the
accusation of blackmailing, he showed that the proposal
came to him from Nicolai, Lange's intimate friend and
ally, and absolutely denied that he had ever dreamt of
accepting it. This of course brought Nicolai into the
field, who made a comically ineffective attempt to restore
peace by flattering both combatants, and suggesting that
they should combine their gifts to produce an ideal
translation of Horace. He, and he alone, had made the
questionable proposal to Lange, and he could show no
authority from Lessing to do so. The affair made a
great stir in the literary world, and the "Vade Mecum "
was widely read. It was a powerful and passionate

work, testifying to great learning, fine taste and judgment, and a temper capable of being stirred to a pitch very dangerous to the " decencies of controversy."

The year 1754 was a very productive one with Lessing. Besides some eighty reviews for the *Vossische Zeitung*, and the "Vade Mecum," it saw the publication of the third and fourth volumes of his "Writings," and the first two numbers of a new periodical, *G. E. Lessing's Theatrical Library*, in which the great undertaking he had begun with Mylius, in the *Theatrical Contributions*, was resumed. The third volume of the " Writings " contained four new Vindications—of Horace, of Cardanus, of a misunderstood satire of the seventeenth century named Ineptus Religiosus, and of Cochläus, a malignant enemy of Luther's, whom Lessing defends, " but only in a trifle." These Vindications, acute and learned as they are, had an indirect value which much outweighed the importance of anything actually established by them. They showed how much new light could be thrown by original research on questions supposed to be long ago set at rest, they stimulated that healthy dislike to taking opinions on trust which Lessing's old schoolmaster had taught him was the beginning of true knowledge, and they had a charm of style which showed learned writers the way to bring the results of their culture before a much larger public than they had ever thought of writing for before. The fourth volume of the " Writings " contained two dramas, " The Young Scholar," and " The Jews."

His work as a translator still went on. He published in 1754, with an introduction, an enlarged edition of a translation by Mylius of Hogarth's "Analysis of Beauty," a work rather ridiculed in England, but of which Lessing saw the philosophic value. The *Theatrical Library* contained long extracts from the Spanish and French drama. Lessing knew that no man of letters can turn his gifts to better use than by winning for the worthy productions of foreign literatures the right of citizenship in his own. In his day Germany was so poor in acquisitions of this kind, that he bitterly complained of the mean idea posterity would have to form of the power of the human spirit in literature if every language save German were to be suddenly destroyed. To-day there is certainly no language which, from this point of view at least, the world could so ill afford to lose; and it is not the least of Lessing's titles to honour that he evoked the spirit which led to this momentous change.

The year 1755 was greeted by Lessing with an ode on Frederick the Great, whose professed and practical recognition of kingship as a "glorious servitude" excited his deep enthusiasm. He now seemed to have fairly taken root in Berlin. He had a publisher who knew his worth; his work, and the tools for it, lay ready to his hand; and he had attracted to himself a large circle of friends. Mendelssohn has already been mentioned; he had also made the acquaintance of Gleim, the wealthy and influential secretary to the Chapter at Halberstadt, known also as an excellent lyrist, and shortly about to be better known as the author of the "Songs of a Prussian Grenadier." In Gleim's company he also met for the first time the only other friend whom he seems to have regarded with the same tenderness of affection which he felt for Mendelssohn—Christian Ewald von Kleist. Kleist was the "Poet of the Spring," so called from his famous descriptive poem, "Der Frühling" (after Thomson), a work of high merit, which was one of the first symptoms of the new renascence.

But a deep restlessness characterized Lessing all his life, and he now began to grow tired of Berlin. There seems to be really no other reason for his departure, which took place in October, 1755, than this ; unless, indeed, his interest in the theatre had been re-awakened by the passing visit of a company of players to Berlin, and he was anxious to renew his acquaintance with the Leipzig stage. Before leaving Berlin, however, he produced something which restored the balance between his creative and his critical activity—the latter having of late decidedly outweighed the former both in quality and quantity. The first number of the *Theatrical Library* had contained a discussion of a novel form of the drama which had appeared on the French stage, the "pathetic comedy," or, as it was satirically called, *comédie larmoyante ;* and had promised one on the analogous innovation on the English stage, the tragedy of middle-class life. The French, says Lessing, "thought that the world had laughed and hooted at vulgar vices long enough in its comedies : it occurred to them, therefore, that the world might now be made to weep in them, and find an elevated pleasure in the representation of quiet virtues." The English, on the other hand, "thought it unjust that our terror and sympathy should be awakened only by rulers and persons of high rank ; they accordingly began to seek for heroes out of the ranks of the *bourgeoisie,* and bound on their feet the tragic buskins in which they had never been seen before, except for purposes of ridicule." [1] The promised treatise on the *tragédie bourgeoise* was never written, but instead of it came an example of the style in question. Lessing's theoretical investigations had as usual led him to verify his conclusions by experiment. He lived from January to the middle of March in great seclusion in a villa at Potsdam, putting the finishing touches to his " Miss Sara Sampson," the first example of its kind in the German language. The title indicates his now clear and fixed intention to make his countrymen aware that the English stage offered them models more congenial than the French. And the plot of the play is clearly traceable to two English works— " Clarissa Harlowe," a novel whose significance and excellence were fully appreciated by Lessing, and Lillo's drama, "The London Merchant." Lessing's heroine, the daughter of an English clergyman, leaves her home with her lover Mellefont, who is sincerely attached to her, but dislikes the idea of marriage, and puts her off with the plea that his marriage at that moment will deprive him of an expected inheritance. A former mistress, Marwood, seeks him out, and finding herself wholly unable to regain his affections, contrives to poison her rival just as Sara's father arrives to bring her forgiveness and hope ; and Mellefont kills himself on her corpse. The play is deeply pathetic, and Sara's sweetness and unselfishness are very sympathetically

[1] Cf. Epictetus, *Diss.* I. xxiv., "remember that tragedies have their place among the wealthy and kings and tyrants, but no poor man fills a part in a tragedy except as one of the chorus."

drawn—still more sympathetically, perhaps, the fierce
and ruthless energy of Marwood. But there is a want of
adequate motive for some of the cardinal decisions of the
hero and heroine, and the action is needlessly encumbered
with reflexions and digressions. But with all its faults
"Sara" shows that Lessing was capable of grappling successfully with the greater problems of dramatic art; and
as a piece of pioneering work in a new region, its effects,
both ethical and æsthetic, were very great. Goethe names
it as one of the powerful influences of its time in increas-
ing the self-respect of the middle classes, and nourishing
that feeling which found its central utterance in the
doctrine of the Rights of Man.

It was acted for the first time at Frankfurt on the
Oder in 1755, and Lessing attended the performance.
The audience, wrote the poet Ramler, who was present,
to Gleim, "sat like statues and wept!"

Another important work which falls within the period
of Lessing's second residence in Berlin, is an essay
entitled "Pope a Metaphysician," written in colla-
boration by himself and Mendelssohn. It was suggested by the theme for a prize offered by the Berlin
Academy for the best essay on Pope's sentence, "Whatever is is right," regarded in connexion with the Leibnitzian theory that this is the best of all possible worlds.
The authors point out that "Whatever is is *right*" is not
the same thing as "Whatever is is *good*," as the reference
to Leibnitz would seem to suggest; and maintain that it is
wholly improper to regard a poet as a metaphysician at
all. He may embody in artistic form the conclusions
which philosophers have reached, as Pope did those of

Shaftesbury, but if we treat him as an original thinker, and look for philosophic systems in his works, we shall be placing ourselves at a point of view which will dis- tort everything we see. Here, as everywhere in Lessing, we find him searching for the true function of the thing he is considering, for the work its nature fits it to do, and forbidding its confusion with things that are essentially alien to it.

Towards the middle of October, 1755, after rejecting, though with hesitation, an offer that reached him from the new University of Moscow, Lessing started for Leipzig, the scene of his first triumphs and trials. "Miss Sara Sampson " was now on the boards of nearly every theatre in Germany, and his fame both as poet and critic was solidly established. All over Germany he was loved, admired, feared, anything but disregarded. He had fitted himself for half a dozen different careers, and no man, not even himself, could tell which he would choose to abide in. As a matter of fact he chose none of them; for, pioneer as he was in many regions, he settled nowhere; his restless energy drove him ever to new explorations, and it was left for other men to build and sow and reap in the clearings hewn by his giant arm.

CHAPTER VIII.

LESSING found his friend Koch, an excellent actor, presiding over the Leipzig stage; and was soon as deep in the society of the players, and in theatrical affairs of all kinds, as in his old Leipzig days. He found his old friend Weisse there; still, like himself writing plays, but writing them with a fatal facility—a man, Lessing thought, who might do something worthy if his work could only be made harder for him. Lessing loved the social life of the tavern, and was not fastidious about his company, caring little for his dignity because, as Goethe observes, he felt himself strong enough to reassume it at any moment he chose. Mendelssohn heard so much of his constant association with the actors that he even wrote to remonstrate on the subject—he thought Lessing should have been developing his talent in retirement instead of in a life so full of distraction, and in company so frivolous. He was wrong; plays written in the closet alone mostly remain there, and Lessing meant his for the stage. He soon began to adapt certain of the comedies of Goldoni for Koch, and some part of the first was even printed; but a new path soon opened before him for which even the theatre was deserted.

He had long cherished the hope of some day seeing foreign countries, especially Italy. And now in Leipzig he made the acquaintance of a young gentleman, son of a wealthy Leipzig tradesman named Winkler, who desired to start on an extensive tour, and invited Lessing to accompany him. Lessing gladly accepted Winkler's proposal, which secured him a salary of three hundred thalers a year, with all expenses of the journey, including board and lodging; and their departure was fixed for Easter, 1756. The journey was intended to last for about three years, and Holland, England, France, and Italy, were to be visited. To prepare himself to turn his journey to the greatest possible profit was now Lessing's main object, and as he found himself greatly deficient in knowledge of art, he began, with the invaluable assistance of Professor Christ (now Rector of the University), those studies in the plastic arts of antiquity with which his fame is so signally associated. A student of art in Leipzig will find his way to Dresden. Lessing did so, and, to his great delight, found his parents there, whom he had not seen for so many years. He returned with them to Kamenz, and promised to pay them another visit, before his departure with Winkler. A token of the visit, in the shape of a pane of glass from the house of his cousin, Theophilus Lessing, of Hoyerswerda, with a Latin sentence scratched on it by Lessing's hand,[1] is still preserved at Kamenz. The Pastor had at last been fairly reconciled to his son's unsettled way of

---

[1] Nunquam ego neque pecunias neque tecta magnifica neque opes neque imperia in bonis. (Never have I counted wealth or splendid mansions or power or dominion among things that are good.) .

life.   Lessing had kept him fully supplied with his publications; he knew how to appreciate them—he saw them praised by men whom he respected not for learning alone, and was content.   To show that he could do something to please even his puritanical sister Dorothea, Lessing now translated the "Serious Call" of William Law, and had it published, with a preface, in Leipzig.

The journey suffered various postponements and changes of plan, Winkler turning out to be a person of very vacillating character; but at last, on May 10, 1756, the travellers got fairly started.   They proceeded in a leisurely fashion to Holland, visiting Gleim at Halberstadt, exploring the treasures of art in the museum at Brunswick, and of literature in the library of Wolfenbüttel, with which latter Lessing was destined to be better acquainted.   In Hamburg Lessing found the greatest German actor of the day, Konrad Eckhoff, to whom he bore an introduction from Weisse, and whose acting, to Eckhoff's gratification, he much admired.   By the end of July they had reached Amsterdam, whence they meant to make expeditions to various Dutch towns, starting for England in October.   But England Lessing was never to see, and the journey he had looked forward to so eagerly was suddenly cut short.   On August 29th Frederick the Great, to the consternation of Europe, anticipated the onslaught of Saxony and Austria, which he knew to be in preparation, and suddenly invaded the former country in order to make it his centre of operations against Bohemia.   Leipzig and Dresden were speedily occupied, and the Saxon army shut up in the Elbe valley near Pirna.   Winkler came to the creditable determination that these were no times for a Saxon gentleman to amuse himself with foreign travel, and, although peace was expected very shortly, at once hurried back to Leipzig; Lessing of course, with what vexation we may imagine, following in his train.

Lessing was Prussian at heart, the cause of Prussia being fundamentally that of reason and liberty, and Leipzig soon became very disagreeable to him. Koch and his company had departed; and what between the distractions entailed by the military occupation of the city, the uncertainty of Winkler's plans, and the prolonged ill-health into which he now fell, Lessing found himself unable to turn to any steady work. He longed to return to Berlin, but as no one expected that the war so suddenly begun would last for seven years, the journey with Winkler was understood to be only postponed for a short time. So he endeavoured to make the best of his position till the war should end, corresponding with Nicolai and Mendelssohn on Aristotle and the laws of the drama, translating Richardson's Æsop, continuing his studies on the Fable, and by personal intercourse endeavouring to influence for good whatever rising dramatic talent he found about him.

For the discomforts which the war entailed on him and the rest of Leipzig, he soon found compensation. Kleist, the "Poet of the Spring," who had been present at the surrender of the Saxon army at Pirna, was thence sent to winter quarters at Zittau, and afterwards, to his intense disgust, instead of being sent on active service to Bohemia, was transferred, with the rank of major, to one of the regiments of occupation in Leipzig.

Here he at once fell sick of influenza, and in Lessing's constant visits their previous acquaintance grew into the warmest friendship. On Kleist's recovery they made many expeditions into the country on horse and foot, " auf die Bilderjagd," on the hunt for poetic images, as they would say; and the phrase, probably invented by Lessing in genial mockery of his friend's love for Nature, soon became the badge of a school. Certainly a pair of noble souls more different than these two could scarcely be imagined—Kleist romantic and often melancholy, loving the poetry of woods and skies and fields, hoping for a hero's death under the flag of Frederick— Lessing cheerful, disputatious, philosophic, most at home among books or in the stimulating social life of the tavern or theatre.

In Kleist's company, Lessing came into contact with many Prussian officers (among others with that General von Tauentzien, whose secretary he afterwards became), and naturally his intimacy with this class, together with his unconcealed admiration for Frederick the Great, did not improve his position in Leipzig society. Frederick had laid the city under a crushing contribution of 90,000 thalers, and the animosity to Prussia was intensely bitter. Winkler shared it to the full, and as Lessing was at this time living in Winkler's house, the relations between them naturally grew very strained. At last Winkler announced that Lessing's engagement must be considered as definitely at an end. Lessing's inter- course with his Prussian friends had certainly been carried on in a needlessly indiscreet way—once, for ex- ample, he had brought a number of them as his guests to the restaurant where he, Winkler, and other Saxons used to dine—but, in fact, his relations with Winkler were such as one like Lessing, who was so little inclined to obey restraints imposed either by conventionality or self-interest, should never have entered into. At any rate, he now found himself suddenly cut adrift, Winkler refusing to make any compensation for his clear breach of contract, at a time when, on the credit of the engagement, Lessing had contracted serious pecuniary obligations. Added to this, his family at Kamenz had begun to feel the terrible drain which Frederick's necessities inflicted on Saxony, and made urgent appeals to him for help. His position was a very painful one. Kleist did his best, and endeavoured, but in vain, to secure some post in Prussian service for one whom he thought it a calamity for Prussia to lose this opportunity of acquiring. Mendelssohn, to whom alone he revealed the depth of his embarrassment, helped him out of his immediate needs with a loan of sixty thalers. Fortunately (at the urgent instance of a friend), he had had his contract with Winkler drawn up in legal form, and he now commenced an action for damages against him; but this, though in the end successful, proved a very lengthy and vexatious proceeding. Well might he say, as he did in a letter to Nicolai, "I am fit for nothing that needs peace and collectedness of mind."

His interest in his friends' work was, however, as keen as ever, and he soon became acquainted with some that deserved his interest in a very unusual degree. Nicolai had begun to bring out through a Leipzig firm a periodical, named a *Library of the Arts and Letters*, with the editing of which Lessing was engaged. Its second number contained the first of a series of war-songs, "by a Prussian Grenadier," with a warm recommendation from Lessing. The Prussian Grenadier was Gleim. In that age of inflated odes, watery epics, and imitative lyrics, the rude, familiar, powerful style of the Grenadier's war-songs was felt by Lessing, Kleist, and their friends to be a most wholesome literary influence. Nor was their influence only literary. In their vivid picturing of the great contemporary events in which German valour played so memorable a part, they afforded just the nourishment that was needed to the growing national feeling of Germany.

In October, 1757, Frederick passed through Leipzig, and we may imagine with what thoughts Lessing saw him single out Gottsched for honour as the most illustrious representative of German literature. Gottsched suffered for it, for Lessing henceforth redoubled his efforts to show him for the pompous futility he was. Frederick did not much need to be shown it ; he probably despised Gottsched even as much as Lessing did, but he was not and would not be made aware that Germany had ever produced anything worthier than Gottsched. Yet so mighty was the personality of the great king that his very contempt served German literature perhaps as well as his favour would have done : it stimulated men to show that they did not deserve it.

Since his breach with Winkler, Lessing had been in a very despondent mood ; but his spirits at last began to rise again. He resumed both study and production. It was doubtless a good sign of reviving energy that he emitted, early in 1758, a flash of the indignation which the maltreatment of classical writers was wont to arouse in him. One Herr Lieberkühn, a Prussian army chaplain, had complained to Nicolai that *his* war-songs "by a Prussian Officer" had, in the *Library*, been pronounced inferior to those of a mere grenadier ! " If he ever takes in hand to write a war-song again," said Lessing, on hearing of this remonstrance, " he shall run the gauntlet for it, though he set it down to a field-marshal." He did indeed have to run the gauntlet for the translation of Theocritus which he now published. Nicolai found Lessing's attack "too malicious." It was certainly very painful reading for Lieberkühn ; but, if a man will undertake to translate Theocritus who "knows less Greek than Gottsched —— ! "

Dramatic aims also occupied him again, and he now wrote a good part of the tragedy of " Emilia Galotti," intending to submit it for a prize offered by Nicolai in the *Library*. He spoke of his project to Nicolai, as though the play were the work of a young friend in whom he was interested :—

. . . " Meantime my young tragedian is getting forward, and my vanity leads me to hope much good from him, for he works much as I do. He writes seven lines in seven days, constantly enlarges his plan, and constantly strikes out something of what has been already finished. . . . He has laid out the play for only three acts, and he uses without hesitation all the liberties of the English stage."

Kleist was stimulated by Lessing to write his drama " Seneca "; and perhaps to some extent forgot, in this new literary activity, the consuming bitterness of soul with which he found himself chained to Leipzig, in charge of a military hospital, while his countrymen were conquering at Rossbach and Leuthen.

It was Lessing's wont to make anything that interested him the starting-point of a critical investigation that often led him very far afield. The Prussian Grenadier had set him, in one direction, upon the study of Tyrtæus and the war poetry of antiquity ; in another, upon the ancient heroic poetry of Germany, the " Heldenbuch," and the " Nibelungenlied," of which latter the first modern edition had just been published by Bodmer. He was deeply impressed with the power of this forgotten national literature, and it never ceased to occupy him ; though, unhappily, his plans for making it better known did not get beyond the stage of notes and *collectanea*.

Early in April Kleist's regiment received the long-expected order to march on active service.

" I feel as if I were in heaven," he wrote to Gleim, to whom he committed a sum of money to keep for him. " I do not think that I shall fall ; however, it is possible. In that case, please give the 200 reichsthalers, which are over and above the 1,000, to Herrn Ramler and Lessing, half to each. Or, rather, give it to them at once ; if I live they can pay me as soon as they have plenty of money."

Leipzig in Kleist's absence would have been scarcely endurable for Lessing. The state of his action against Winkler now permitted him to leave it, and on the 4th of May he started for Berlin. A week later Kleist marched with his regiment to Zwickau, and the friends, who had found each other so lately, never met again.

CHAPTER IX

L ESSING'S third residence in Berlin, which lasted about three years and a half, was a period of strenuous literary activity. His researches in Old German literature were eagerly carried on, with the assistance of the poet Ramler, who now joined the circle of his intimate friends. Nor was the drama neglected:—

"Herr Ramler and I make project after project. Only wait a quarter of a century, my dear Gleim, and you will be amazed at all we shall have written. Particularly I. I write day and night, and my smallest resolve at present is to make at least three times as many dramas as Lope de Vega. I shall very soon have my 'Doctor Faust' played here. Come soon again to Berlin, so that you may see it."

Lessing had seen the " Volkscomödie " of " Doctor Faust " represented by Schuch's company in Berlin, in 1755, and had discussed with Mendelssohn a plan for turning it into a *tragédie bourgeoise*. The Devil was to be got rid of, and his place taken by a human "archvillain." In another scheme, of which an interesting fragment remains, it was intended, say the Herrn von Blankenburg and Engel, to whom Lessing had talked of his plan, to cheat Mephistopheles of his prey by showing him that he had had to do with a mere phantom-Faust, created to afford a warning to the real Faust, in whose mind the whole drama is supposed to have been transacted in a dream. It was a time in which, as Herr von Blankenburg observes, all the poets in Germany were writing "Fausts," and Lessing had felt deeply the impressiveness of the wild legend. Faust was a type of adventure, of dauntless exploration into the secrets of the universe; and the age eagerly accepted him as the incarnation of its spirit. But having done so, it clearly could not deliver him over to perdition; he might be warned, tried, punished, but in the end he must be saved; and we see that Lessing, as well as Goethe, though in a much less subtle and artistic fashion, observes this new ethical necessity in the treatment of the theme.

One of the many projects entertained by Ramler and Lessing was an edition of the epigrams, or "Sinngedichte," of Logau, a then almost unknown poet of the seventeenth century, who has since become a German classic. Lessing, after driving Ramler to the verge of frenzy by his desultory ways of working (he had just then "ten irons in the fire at once"), did at last furnish an introduction and glossary, and Logau was published in Leipzig, 1759.

The Prussian Grenadier's lyrics were also now collected and edited by Lessing. Some of the later of them had exhibited a tone of vindictiveness and hatred which he found unworthy of his friend, and he made his complaint to Gleim very frankly. Prussian in sympathy as he was, the notion of national enmities invading literature was intensely repugnant to him.

" I have," he even went so far as to say, " no conception at all of the love of country, and it seems to me at best a heroic failing which I am well content to be without."

A hard saying certainly for many of Lessing's admirers, but it is not difficult to reconcile oneself to such a *saying* from a man who was German of the Germans in every trait of mind and character, and who did more than any contemporary towards forming and fortifying the national sentiment. He might well refuse to triumph with Prussia over Saxony, but it was with no cosmopolitan indifference that he read Gleim's pæan on the epoch-making victory at Rossbach :

" What would I not give if one could translate the whole song into French ! It would make the wittiest Frenchman as much ashamed of himself as if they had lost the battle of Rossbach a second time."

The objectionable passages in Gleim were altered in Lessing's sense.

The autumn of 1758 saw the beginning of a most important literary undertaking. Nicolai, Lessing, and Mendelssohn had for some time been meditating the establishment of a new periodical which should discuss literary questions in that tone of conversational ease which suited Lessing's dramatic genius so excellently. According to Nicolai the immediate impulse to the enterprise was given by the appearance of a publication in which they found much that called for condemnation —perhaps the "Critical and Satirical Writings " of one Dusch, which contained, in the form of a corre-spondence, a hostile criticism on " Miss Sara Sampson "

and the *Theatrical Library.* " Let us suppose,"
suggested Lessing, "that Kleist has been slightly
wounded, and that we are addressing a weekly batch
of letters to him." This was the origin of the feared
and famous *Litteraturbriefe*—letters on contemporary
literature which appeared weekly for the next seven
years, and to which Lessing contributed much excellent
and influential criticism. Lessing, Mendelssohn, and
Nicolai, were the only contributors, though each used
various signatures, and the identity of the authors was
intended to be kept profoundly secret. In the first
year of the periodical Lessing contributed more than
two-thirds of the Letters, and his influence is felt in
the manner and substance of all of them. Goethe
and Schiller, however, thought that there were certain
signs by which the hand of the " Proctophilosoph "
could be discerned :—

" Nicolai also wrote in the excellent work ? Very likely.
Many a commonplace, too, stands in the excellent work." [1]

The *Litteraturbriefe* naturally invite comparison with
the earlier letters which form the second volume of
Lessing's "Writings." They show a very striking
advance. The fire, the wit, the wonderful mastery
of style, the unerring recognition of all that is pre-
tentious or commonplace in the works reviewed, and
the scathing satire that punished it—these qualities, all
indicated in the earlier letters, are fully ripened in the
later ones. Their influence on German literature, over
the whole field of which they freely ranged, was very

[1] " *Zahme Xenien.*" Goethe and Schiller.

powerful. Complacent mediocrity, arrogant pedantry, were scourged from the field, true genius was summoned to fill it, and the nation's mind and taste were educated to recognize it when it came. Everywhere they aroused, inspired, showed the path of advance. One of the earlier letters, in criticizing certain translations of Pope, Bolingbroke, and Gay, points to the great deficiency of German literature in this field, then occupied only by drudges who could occupy no other. Another summons a new race of historians to take the place of the clever writers who will not study, and the learned ones who cannot write. Others deal with popular poetry in Germany and elsewhere—others continue Lessing's lifelong war upon Gottsched and his school, who occasionally fire off a shot in return with much smoke and noise, and very little metal. Shakspere is upheld as the true and congenial model for the German drama. Wieland comes in for some sharp criticism on the subject of his drama, " Lady Jane Grey," imitated, without acknowledgment, from Rowe. Religious and philosophic literature was also taken thought of, and a religious periodical, the *Northern Guardian*, in whose management Klopstock had a large part, is handled at much length and with great severity for endeavouring to make up by a copious religious phraseology for its lack of solid and sincere thought. The seventeenth Letter criticizes the old popular drama of " Faust," in which Lessing finds scenes conceived with a " Shaksperean power," and, apropos of this, communicates the powerful fragment of Lessing's own " Faust," which is all we now possess of his play. It represents Faust in his study,

questioning as to their swiftness a number of spirits
whom he has evoked.   At last one declares that he is as
swift "as the change from good to evil."   " Ha! thou
art my devil !   As the change from good to evil?   I
have felt how swift that is !—I have felt it ! "

On August 12, 1759, Lessing then deep in his cam-
paign against the *Northern Guardian*, the " Poet of the
Spring" was fighting other Northerns of a much sterner
quality.   It was the disastrous day of Kunnersdorf, the
worst defeat the Prussian arms had ever suffered under
Frederick's flag.   All looked hopeful at first—Kleist
and his men had taken three batteries, he was hurt,
but never thought of retiring.   At last he was badly hit
in both arms; at the same moment his colonel fell ;
Kleist sprang into his place and led the regiment
forward up the deadly slopes of sand.   But the turning-
point of the battle was reached—the Russian fire grew
heavier and closer, and Kleist fell, his leg broken
by a cannon shot.   "My children," he cries, "don't
forsake your king ! "   But neither he nor they can do
anything more ; the Russian tide rolls irresistibly back,
the Prussian ranks melt away in ruinous flight,—and
for the hapless Poet of the Spring even the hero's
death is not yet come.   A surgeon tried to bind his
wounds, but was blown to pieces at his side, and in
the evening a party of savage Cossacks plundered him
lying helpless there, stripped him naked, and flung
him into a swamp.   A second time this happened,
after some Russian hussars had given him clothing
and bread.   At last, on the 13th, he was found by
a party of Russian cavalry, among whom was a kindly

German named Falkelberg, conveyed to Frankfurt, and lodged in the house of Professor Nicolai,[1] where all was done for him that man could do. But all was useless, and after lingering some ten days, he died. It was his country's blackest hour, yet even then the loss of so noble and gifted a nature was sorely felt. But few had such cause to mourn him as Lessing, who had been on the point of starting to take charge of him when the news of his death arrived.

" Ah, dearest friend," he wrote to Gleim, " it is too true. He is dead. We have lost him. He died in the house and in the arm s of Professor Nicolai. Even when in the greatest pain he was always tranquil and cheerful. He longed much to see his friends again. Had it only been possible ! My grief for this event is a very wild grief. I do not ask, indeed, that the bullets should turn aside because a good man stands there ; but I do ask that the good man—— See, my pain often leads me into anger with the man himself for whom I suffer. He had already three, four wounds ; why did he not retire ? For fewer and slighter wounds Generals have left the front without disgrace. He *would* die. Forgive me if I am too hard on him ; for it may well be that I am too hard on him. He would not have died even of the last wound, they say, but he was neglected. Neglected ! I know not against whom I must rage. Wretches, that neglected him !— Ha, I must stop. The Professor has doubtless written to you. He has delivered an oration on him. Somebody else, I do not know who, has written a threnody on him. They cannot have lost much in Kleist who are now able to do such things. The Professor will have his oration printed—and it is so wretched ! I know well that Kleist would rather have carried another wound to his grave than have such stuff chattered after him. Has a Professor a heart ?

---

[1] A brother of Lessing's friend. The other brother, the Nicolai who was concerned in the Lange controversy, had died in September, 1758.

Now he wants verses from me and Ramler, to have printed with his oration. If he should ask this from you too, and you fulfil his desire——! Dearest Gleim, you must not do it. You feel too much at present to say what you feel. And it is not the same thing to you as it is to a Professor, what you say and how you say it. Farewell. I shall write more to you when I am quieter."

Lessing would not contribute to the Professor's elegiac volume, but when in later days a monument was erected to Kleist he wrote an epigram on the subject, which is perhaps the best he ever produced :—

> " This stone in memory, Kleist, of thee ?
> Thou wilt the stone's memorial be ! "

Lessing had pursued his studies in the Fable very zealously, and in October, 1759, he brought out a volume of fables, in three books, with the treatise on the subject which we have already mentioned appended to it. He was also studying Greek literature, and even collecting materials for a Life of Sophocles, whose value as a dramatic model he thought very highly of. This plan came to nothing, but in its stead came a drama in the austere Greek manner named " Philotas " ; the hero of which is a young Greek prince, who kills himself in captivity to secure his country's triumph against the enemy. This drama contrasts strongly with " Miss Sara Sampson " in he simplicity and firmness of its outline, everything being pruned away that does not tend to the development of the action. Besides the Greek drama we find him now also powerfully attracted by the plays and dramatic criticisms of Diderot—"the most philosophic mind," he wrote, in an introduction to a translation of

them published by him in 1760, " which has concerned
itself with the drama since Aristotle." Lessing certainly
gained much from Diderot, and acknowledged it fully.
The language of his dramas grew from henceforth more
natural and simple ; their action developed itself less
obviously in accordance with a preconceived idea, and
more in obedience to character and circumstance ; his
best play, " Minna von Barnhelm," is an admirable
example of that *genre sérieux*—the *genre sérieux* treated
with a tender and sympathetic humour—which Diderot
summoned rising dramatists to cultivate. From Diderot
too Lessing learned to realize the great importance of
the part which moral character must play in the production of a good drama. " Study ethics," he wrote
afterwards to his brother Karl, who was also beginning
to write comedies—" study ethics, learn to express
yourself well and accurately, and cultivate your own
character." [1]

Frederick's affairs went steadily to ruin in the year
1760, since Kunnersdorf ; and, on October 9th, the
Russians and Austrians, after ten hours' bombardment,
entered and to some extent plundered Berlin. Lessing
had now lived in that city almost as long as he ever
cared to live in one place ; he may have suffered losses
at the hands of the invaders, and for other reasons he
was anxious for a change. In his usual silent fashion,
taking leave of no human being, he departed from Berlin
in November, 1760. After a visit to Kleist's grave at

---

[1] " Voulez-vous être auteur? Voulez-vous être critique? Com-
mencez par être homme de bien," etc. Diderot : *De la Poésie
aramatique*, xxii.

Frankfurt-on-the-Oder, we next find him, not without surprise, established in Breslau as secretary to General von Tauentzien, now Commandant of that town, which he had lately defended with great skill and valour against the Austrians. Tauentzien had also been made Director of the Mint, a most lucrative post, if one chose to make it so, by the opportunities it gave of profiting by the continual debasement of the coinage which Frederick was obliged to have recourse to. Lessing had made his acquaintance in Kleist's company at Leipzig, and respected and liked him for his soldierlike frankness and faith. "If Frederick were brought so low," he said once, "that his army could be assembled under a single tree, General Tauentzien would be under that tree."

CHAPTER X

L ESSING, in a garrison town, with little in the way of literary society, with new acquaintances and new employments, found himself after a time much disposed to regret his change. Regret, indeed, is hardly the word for his feelings; he writes of his position to Ramler and Mendelssohn in a tone of bitterness and dejection which can hardly be attributed solely to his sorrowful recollection of that "Klubb" in Berlin, "where every night I could eat my fill, drink my fill, and quarrel my fill—especially quarrel about things I did not understand." He longed to return, "but can one retrieve one inconsiderate step by another?" He sought relief in whatever distraction the place afforded, and he found it, such as it was, in the theatre of Breslau, where the old harlequinades attacked by Gottsched, but not at all disliked by Lessing, were much in vogue. He went much also into the company of Prussian officers, a class whose society was always pleasant to him. Here, however, the great feature of the social gatherings in which he was wont to spend long hours of the night, was faro, and Lessing became a passionate and confirmed gambler. No catastrophe ever came of it; he often won, and he declared that the excitement of play, which he felt intensely, was a necessity for his health—it set the blood in motion and relieved a certain sense of lethargy even then sometimes perceived by him, which was a very marked feature in the illness that ended his life. At all times, it appears, he had the enviable gift of being able to sink into a profound and dreamless sleep whenever he chose to close his eyes.

The relations at Kamenz were delighted with the new move. Their son had at last a post, an *Amt*; how much preferable was this to the hand-to-mouth life of a mere author! And a profitable *Amt*, too, though not so profitable as it might have been had Lessing taken advantage of his position as secretary to the Director of the Mint, and indulged in the speculations of dubious honesty by which even Tauentzien amassed a large fortune. There were Jews, too, not of the Mendelssohn stamp, who would have made it worth his while to give them an occasional hint of Frederick's intentions respecting the coinage. But he had a fine sense of honour, and a fine indifference to "riches and mansions, power and dominion," which brought him unstained through this rather dangerous ordeal. His salary, indeed, was ample, and his relatives rejoiced at it. Already he had now and again pinched himself to help them, for their distress had been for some time very great, partly owing to the impoverishment caused by the war, partly to the growing unpopularity of the pastor, whose puritanical severity was bearing fruit in a rather malignant reaction against his influence. Lessing responded to their new appeals as well as he could—not so well as he might have done had he not been Lessing. It was his habit to spend money as he got it; he had generally a floating debt, which had to be kept afloat, and he never refused a request for alms. He would plunge his hand into his pocket, and bestow whatever came out, gold or silver, on the petitioner. "You help the undeserving," was said to him. "*Ach Gott!*" replied Lessing, "what should we have if we all got only what we deserve?" This was generous; but could he not have controlled his generosity sometimes in order to be more generous to those entirely deserving people at Kamenz, who had considerable claims on him too—a father who had lately submitted to a great loss rather than drag a fraudulent fellow-clergyman before the Courts? Surely, one must answer; but if one has no sense of thrift for oneself it is not so easy to have it for others. Lessing's money did not, however, go altogether in alms and faro. He made use of it to collect an excellent library, and by the time he left Breslau had about 6,000 volumes, including some early and rare editions of the Classics, and much patristic literature.

The Fathers engaged his attention much in this Breslau period, and he laid the foundation here of that knowledge of ecclesiastical history of which he showed such astonishing mastery in the controversies of his later days. Spinoza also he now began to study profoundly, and this period is one of great importance in the progress of his religious opinions. In his "Thoughts on the Herrnhuter" (1750) he had praised that sect for its exaltation of religious practice over theological specu-lation. In his fragment, "On the Origin of Revealed Religion" (*circ.* 1755), he had argued that positive religions

7

all sprang simply from the desire to draw up for universal
acceptance a body of truths such as every man if left to
himself would discover, but discover in degrees of com-
pleteness varying according to his own natural capacities.
Every man would formulate his own natural religion
differently; and the effort to find a common formula
inevitably led to the introduction of much that was
erroneous. Even thus, for example, natural justice
has been codified into laws which contain much that
is fallible and conventional. Apparently under the
influence of Spinoza and the Fathers, this attitude of
philosophic toleration towards revealed religion now
changed to deep hostility and contempt. Such at least is
the impression left on the reader's mind by Lessing's essay
" On the Manner of the Propagation and Extension of
the Christian Religion," composed during his residence
at Breslau, in which the early Christian Churches are coldly
compared in various points with the licentious Bacchana-
lian associations in Rome, whose abolition is described
by Livy.[1]   However, as he wrote to Mendelssohn about
ten years later, he soon found that in "getting rid
of certain prejudices" he had also thrown away something which he would have to recover. " That I have
not in part done so already, is only due to my fear lest,
by degrees, I should drag the whole rubbish into the
house again." A fragment, which shall be communicated
in the place to which it seems to belong, shows, if we
date it rightly, that this process of recovery had made
considerable way before the end of Lessing's life.

---

[1] None of these works was published in Lessing's lifetime.

In February, 1763, it became the duty of the Governor's secretary—a duty which Lessing performed with extreme good-will—to publicly proclaim to Breslau the Peace of Hubertsburg. Tauentzien now became Governor of all Silesia, and Lessing had hopes, which, however, were not fulfilled, of receiving some higher and more lucrative post. Meantime his official work became lighter, and he had more leisure for thought and production. Soon, indeed, there came a period of enforced leisure which seems to have had a marked effect on his intellectual development. He was struck down by a dangerous fever in the summer of 1764, and his convalescence was slow. But this period of stillness and contemplation, in which death had to be contemplated too, laid on his vehement spirit a touch which brought it the delicacy and serenity it had lacked.

"All changes of temperament," he wrote to Ramler on the 5th of August, "are, I think, connected with operations that take place in our animal organization. The serious epoch of my life is approaching; I am beginning to be a man, and flatter myself that in the heat of this fever I have raved out the last remnant of my youthful follies."

A fortnight later, he wrote to the same friend that he still finds some difficulty in settling to his work again. "A sorry life! when one is up, and yet vegetates; it is looked upon as healthy without being so. Before my illness I was working with such a spirit and energy as I have rarely known. I cannot recall it again, try how I will."

The work on which he had been so pleasantly engaged before his illness, and which he wrote mostly in the little summer-house of his garden, was "Minna von Barn-helm." This noble play was the direct outcome of his life in Breslau ; the story it contains had been, in substance, enacted under his own eyes in the inn " Zum Goldenen Gans." A Prussian officer, Major von Tellheim, for whose character Kleist furnished several traits, has been dismissed at the close of the Seven Years' War, under the imputation of having attempted a fraud on the Prussian War Treasury. The charge was based on an act of generosity towards some Saxon townspeople from whom he had been required to levy, in cash, a cruel war-contribution. He had advanced, from his own means, the sum which he could not bring himself to wring from their necessities, taking their bills in ex-change ; and those bills, which the Prussian War Office should have seen honoured, were looked on there as merely a bribe to Tellheim for having exacted less than he could have done. Tellheim, a man of an almost morbid sense of honour, resolves, while the investigation he has challenged is pending, to have no communication with a wealthy Saxon lady, Minna von Barnhelm, to whom he had become betrothed during the war, and whose interest in him was first awakened by the very act of generosity towards her countrymen for which he is now suffering. Suspecting how the case stands, she seeks him out in Berlin, finds him sunk in want and dejection, and endeavours to remove the scruples which forbid him to link his stained career with hers. But he is unmoved until she tells him that her flight to him has caused her to be disinherited and disowned, and that she is alone and helpless unless he will protect her.

Tellheim's instant revulsion of feeling is now exhibited with exquisite skill, and his endeavours to meet the problems thus forced upon him awaken both our love and our laughter. At this point arrives a letter from the king, who has been investigating Tellheim's case. It admits the justice of his claims, which the Treasury has orders to honour, and with a flattering acknowledgment of his past services, reinstates him in his rank in the Prussian army. It is now Minna's turn to punish him, to his astonishment and dismay, by imitating the petty punctilio which had made him reject her when the worldly advantages of the union had seemed to be all on his side. At last the arrival of the uncle, by whom Minna had fictitiously represented herself to be disowned, puts an end to his distress. This graceful story is worked out through a number of episodes ingeniously and naturally contrived to keep the interest in action and character alive. The construction of the play is almost faultless, and the minor characters—Tellheim's stubbornly faithful soldier-servant, the mean and inquisitive landlord, Minna's vivacious maid, and the rest, are most happily drawn; the types indeed conventional, but the presentation of them full of originality and humour. The manner, too, in which Frederick is introduced—a majestic impersonation of justice, never appearing in the play, but felt in it throughout as a supreme and beneficent influence—forms a noble expression of Lessing's reverence for his great king.

"Minna von Barnhelm" was a literary phenomenon of great significance in its day. It was the Rossbach of German literature—the death-blow of French prestige and influence in that sphere. Lessing himself had rarely ventured hitherto to give German names to the persons in his comedies—so fundamentally unfit for artistic purposes did Germans consider the realities that lay nearest to them. Now for Orontes, Lisettes, Theophans, Damons, we have Tellheim, Werner, Franziska, Minna—we can hardly conceive the state of things in which this was a portent, but such it was. The army had never appeared on the stage before, except as represented by some cowardly braggart : on it, too, Lessing laid his ennobling hand. The Franco-German drama of the "Gottschedianer" was a purely artificial and foreign product. It had refinement, elevation, wit ; but it had absolutely no connection with the life of the German people. But " Minna " was German through and through—events, characters, manners, sentiments ; and on all these was shed that ideal light which the popular and native literature of Germany had theretofore so deeply lacked. Nor is the interest of the play purely literary. The enormous service which the wars of Frederick had rendered towards the solidifying of German national sentiment had been largely annulled by the intense animosity between Saxony and Prussia which had unavoidably arisen in their progress. In Lessing's reconciling drama—the work of one who was Saxon by birth and Prussian by conviction—the grace and spirit of Saxony vanquish the perverse, if honourable, obstinacy of Prussia, and national enmities are lost in individual affections. Never surely did a citizen of one country desert it for another, and a hostile one, with such advantage to both.

All that was effected in "Minna" might, of course, have been conceived by any one, and the times were full of such ideas. But to present them with a power that compelled attention, and dissolved prejudice, was work for a Lessing. Frederick the Great, one laments to find, never could be persuaded to read the greatest German drama of his day; but it was soon read and acted throughout all his dominions and beyond them, and the day when it will cease to be so is not at hand yet. It is true that it contains no profound study of human nature—that even on their own plane of interest the characters impress us rather as manufactures than as creations—that the touches which suggest that they have a life outside of the action of the drama are wanting. But if manufacture, they are the manufacture of a most skilful craftsman, and the play remains a striking proof of how very nearly the results of poetic genius may be attained by a high critical intelligence backed by a moral character of true nobility and refinement. The atmosphere of the play is as wholesome as we can find in literature, and it is written with a genial, sunny power, which tells that it was the fruit of cheerful and hopeful days.

Not only Lessing's best creative, but also (in the sphere of *belles lettres*) his best critical work was mainly produced in Breslau. He had been greatly occupied with antiquarian studies, and especially with the theories advanced by Spence, Count Caylus, and others, as to the relation between the plastic arts and poetry as illustrated in antiquity. The prevailing opinion was that the excellence of a poem was in direct proportion to the number of subjects it afforded for pictorial representation, and that each art found its highest expression in imitating the effects of the other. Nothing could be more contrary to Lessing's general principles of art, and he began to set down his ideas on the subject in his usual way—defining, examining, and confuting the views of various authors in succession, and so advancing towards truth by a method which has all the charm of a dramatic action. While thus engaged, an epoch-making book was published, Winckelmann's "History of Ancient Art"—a work reckoned the primary cause of the movement which soon doubled and trebled the hours given to Greek in all the classical schools of Germany, and made that language what it is now—the basis of her higher culture. Lessing read it with profound delight; but found that Winckelmann had advanced what he considered a false theory as to the period of the execution of the famous Laocoon group. Moreover, in a previous work of Winckelmann's, the same group had been criticized, in connection with the account of the incident given by Virgil, on the assumption that the two arts are fundamentally one in their limits and capacities.

Taking, then, Winckelmann on the Laocoon as his point of departure—a wise choice, for anything he could write on Winckelmann just then was sure of an attentive hearing—he proceeded to develop his views on the general relation of the plastic and literary arts. Lessing shows that the material of the poet is Time, of the artist, Space—the latter represents objects, the former operations, or objects through operations, even as Homer describes the shield of Achilles by telling us how it was made. Then, from the special nature of the material in which it works, Lessing proceeds to deduce in much detail the true conditions and aims of each art. Music, too, and even dancing, were to have been treated in subsequent parts, whereof only some notes and fragments exist ; so that the whole work would have offered a com-plete science of æsthetics.

The first part, that which alone was fully carried out by Lessing, is chiefly concerned with the vital distinctions which exist between poetry and the pictorial arts in their treatment of visible objects or actions. Virgil represents Laocoon as screaming with anguish in the coils of the serpents. But does the sculptured Laocoon scream ? Not at all ; the only sound which his lips can utter is a deep, suppressed groan. Winckelmann appears to reckon this difference to the credit of the sculptor—the latter conceiving his subject in a more heroic and dignified light than the poet. Lessing, of course, has no difficulty in showing that the loudest and most unrestrained ex-pressions of grief or pain were not thought, in antiquity, to be inconsistent with the loftiest heroism. But yet the difference is there—and is it to be set down to mere chance ? By no means. The plastic artist can treat only a single instant in all the life of Laocoon—shall he select and eternalize one in which the features must be so distorted by the wide opening of the mouth as to make every spectator turn away his eyes in disgust ? The end of every art is pleasure ; the plastic arts can gain this end through the representation of beautiful form, and of that alone ; for every ugly thing becomes unendurable when rendered permanent in painting or sculpture. But the poet, on the other hand, is not confined to the representation of the beautiful. Nothing compels him to concentrate his picture in a single instant. He can relate from beginning to end the details of every action of which he treats. He can bring it before us in all its successive changes; and each change, which would cost the artist a separate work, costs him but a single touch. Even though one of these touches, regarded in itself alone, should displease the imagination of the hearer, yet we have been prepared for it by what went before, or the effect is softened by what follows; we cannot isolate it, and in its proper place and connection it may be of the utmost artistic value. Virgil's Laocoon screams, but this screaming Laocoon is the very man whom we have known and loved as the wise patriot, the affectionate father. We refer his *clamores horrendi*, not to his character, but to his unendurable suffering. This suffering is all we hear in his screams, and by these alone could the poet make us realize it.

Again, Poetry and the visual arts each aim at the production of an illusion in the mind of the hearer or spectator. Poetry does this by means of arbitrary signs to which a certain meaning is conventionally attached— viz., letters and words. But Art effects the same end by *natural* signs—signs which really imitate the thing intended to be signified. Let Art, then, recognize its own sphere and abide in it! Its business is to represent the visible by the visible; not, after the fashion of the allegoristic painters, to use line and colour as a sort of handwriting for the conveyance of other things than those which they can directly represent. And Poetry, too—let it remember that if its arbitrary signs are to create illusion, (as they can do by means of rhythm, metaphor, and the skilful handling of language,) they must not be used to give the impression of any object by describing in succession all its parts, by endeavouring to give the effect of Space through the medium of Time. We can see a statue at a glance, but we cannot read at a glance a detailed description of a beautiful face and form; we have forgotten the beginning before we have reached the end, and no total impression remains on the mind. The business of Poetry is action; if it would show us what a thing is like, let it tell us what it *does*. Homer brings the idea of a beautiful woman more vividly before us by telling us how the old men swore, as Helen passed them, that she was worth all the wars that had been waged for her sake, than Ariosto does in his forty lines of minute description of all Alcina's charms.

Not all of Lessing's conclusions have been established. His knowledge of literature, ancient and modern, was vast, and he wielded it with the ease of perfect mastery. But his knowledge of art was far from being equally complete. The museum at Dresden, which contains much that is interesting but little that is great, was the most important collection of antique sculpture that he had seen. The Laocoon he knew only through engravings, and a plaster cast of the head of the principal figure. Painting had never interested him much; he doubted whether the discovery of oil-painting was an advantage to art—he doubted, indeed, whether colour of any kind could compensate for the loss of the greater freedom and spirit which he found in uncoloured drawings. It is not surprising, then, that he should define the object of art too narrowly as the representation of beautiful form. Beauty consists, he asserted, in the harmony of parts—ideal beauty is form deprived of all that mars this harmony. This ideal is most nearly realized in the human body; this, then, is the true subject for the artist. Portraiture has a certain place in art—for a good portrait is not a mere imitation of an individual face, it is the ideal of that individual face. But " the painter of landscapes and flowers " is told that genius has no part in his work—Lessing could not see how one could make an ideal landscape, and where there is no ideal there is no art.

Lessing's efforts, therefore, to point out its true province to art are much less successful than those in which he does the same office for literature. The artist's object is really not other or narrower than the poet's. It is to represent *life*—life in its widest sense, moral or physical, human, animal, or elemental—so far as it can be directly represented by form or colour. Directly represented— this is a sound limitation of Lessing's; and, of course, the fact that the artist has to deal with visual appearances, not scientific realities, and the necessity he is under of choosing but a single instant to portray, will suggest other limitations which only bad taste will violate. But why should the representation of what is ugly or detestable be more strictly forbidden to the artist than to the poet? Both are forbidden to isolate and dwell upon any manifestation of the forces, organic or moral, which make for corruption and death. But both may represent these forces in due contrast and subordination to those which oppose them; and, as a matter of fact, the great schools of art in all lands and ages have taken this liberty without hesitation. Beauty has never been their aim; it has followed them unsought. It will always follow every faithful effort to represent the life of Nature, and can no more be exhaustively defined as proportion in form than as harmony of colour.

But whatever may be said against the soundness of this or that conclusion of Lessing's, the effect of the "Laocoon" was stimulating and illuminating in the highest degree, and it had the immediate and salutary effect of putting an end to the vapid descriptive poetry with which the Swiss school was flooding Germany.

Lessing did not seem likely to rise in the service of General Tauentzien, though we hear of no complaint as to the manner in which he did his duty there. But it was, indeed, something of an anomaly that he should be in it at all. He determined to resign his appointment and leave Breslau; and the question was what next to turn to? He had been offered, while at Breslau, the post of Professor of Oratory at the University of Königsberg— a tempting offer, but it was connected with a condition for him prohibitive. He would have to pronounce every year a laudatory oration on the reigning sovereign. Frederick, indeed, one would gladly laud; but, reflected Lessing, who can tell who may come next? "Who can tell that you will survive him?" might have been answered; but the appointment was declined, and one is not sorry to find that Lessing's praise remained a wholly unpurchasable commodity.

Then his cherished dream of visiting Rome and

Greece revived.   He had saved a little money from his
salary; the Winkler action had lately been decided in
his favour, and he was awarded six hundred thalers (three
hundred of which, however, went in legal expenses).   But
he had debts, too, and on investigation he found that his
means would not stretch enough to permit him to trave
so far to any good purpose.

In his undecided state of mind Berlin naturally
attracted him again, and in May, 1765, after a flying
visit to Leipzig and Kamenz, he revisited that capital,[1]
there to sit for awhile, as he expressed it, " like a bird
on the roof," waiting till something should happen to
direct his further flight.

[1] Here he found Nicolai engaged in a new literary undertaking.
The *Litteraturbriefe*, to which Lessing had of late years contributed
very little, had been discontinued; and Nicolai had founded in its
place a new periodical, the *Allgemeine Bibliothek*, an organ which
soon exercised much influence on public opinion.   Nicolai, although
he had imbibed sound views on one or two topics at a time when
such views were far from common, was a man as dull and stiff in
intellect as any Philistine ; and the application of " common sense "
to literature which distinguished his new journal ultimately caused
Goethe, Schiller, and the Romantic school to make war upon him
as a sort of second Gottsched.   Lessing would have been out of
place as a contributor to the *Allgemeine Bibliothek*, and he held
himself entirely aloof from the enterprise.

CHAPTER XI.

AT Berlin a new and delightful prospect opened itself for a moment before Lessing. The Librarian of the Royal "Schlossbibliothek" had lately died, his place was to fill, and, after negotiations with Winckelmann had been broken off on a question of salary ("A thousand thalers is enough for a German," said Frederick, and Winckelmann would have refused an offer of thrice the sum conveyed in such terms), Col. Guichard, better known as Quintus Icilius, a favourite officer of Frederick's, and a patron of German literature, endeavoured to get the vacancy for Lessing. It is sad to think that Lessing and the great King, each supreme in his own sphere, each working in that sphere for the same common end, the creation of the German nation, should have never come into that friendly contact with each other which would have been so helpful to both. The author thoroughly understood and reverenced the king and his work—the king knew and would know nothing of the author, except what had been told him by a tongue of proved malignity and falsehood. He refused the application of Lessing's friend, and on being again approached on the subject angrily forbade his name to be mentioned, and declared that he would get a librarian for himself from France ; which he accordingly did, in the shape of a M. Pernety, who had certainly the qualification of nationality, but absolutely no other.

It was thought, while Lessing's success was still possible, that it would serve him to bring himself into notice by some learned essay which would prove his fitness for the post. He accordingly took up the "Laocoon," which he had brought with him in a fragmentary and chaotic condition from Breslau, and began, with the help of Mendelssohn, some of whose penetrating criticisms were of great service to Lessing, to prepare it for publication. It appeared in the spring of 1766, and the influence, salutary, if partly misleading, which it at once began to exercise on the ripening intellects of the day may be estimated by the striking passage in which Goethe, in his Autobiography, describes its effect :—

"One must be young to realize what an influence Lessing's 'Laocoon' exercised on us. . . . The so long misunderstood 'Ut pictura, poesis' was at once got rid of, the distinction between the plastic and literary arts was made clear ; the summits of both now appeared separate, however closely their bases might join each other. The plastic artist must keep within the limits of the beautiful, although the writer, by whom nothing that has significance can be spared, may be permitted to travel outside of them. One works for the external sense, which can only be satisfied with the beautiful ; the other for the imagination, which we know will find a way to reconcile itself with what is ugly. Like lightning all the consequences of this splendid thought flashed upon us ; all former criticism was flung away like a worn-out garment."

Winckelmann, who had never heard of Lessing before, read his frank and most respectful criticisms with an admiration which afterwards, unhappily, as the "Lao-coon" grew famous, changed to a feeling of rather unworthy resentment; and he spoke of Lessing in a letter to a friend as a mere "university wit," who wished to distinguish himself by paradoxes—one who had so little knowledge that "no answer would have a meaning for him." Strangely enough, the task was laid on Lessing to edit, after Winckelmann's death, a selection of his letters; he found this one among those from which he had to choose the most important, and he quietly included it in the collection. On hearing of Winckelmann's tragic death, he wrote to Nicolai that this was the second author who had lately died for whom he would gladly have given some years of his own life. The first was Laurence Sterne.

"Minna von Barnhelm" was finished in the autumn of 1766. Ramler had read it with the closest attention, and made numerous suggestions, almost all of which Lessing adopted. It was acted for the first time in Hamburg, in the autumn of 1767, and early in the follow-ing year in Berlin, where it was received with an enthusiasm that soon spread its fame into every part of Germany. Never had any play achieved such a success on the German stage ; never, as Anna Karsch, the poetess, who saw it in Berlin, wrote to Gleim, had any German poet so succeeded in awakening the enthusiasm and delight of "both gentle and simple, learned and unlearned." To actors and managers it brought golden harvests. Lessing himself its many representations never enriched by a single penny.[1]

[1] So says Ramler in a letter to a friend written in 1771.

From his arrival in Berlin till the spring of 1767—
except for a summer's tour to Pyrmont in 1766 in company of a young nobleman, Leopold von Breitenhoff—
Lessing, as he expresses it, stood idle in the market-
place in Berlin waiting for some one to hire him; no
one, apparently, knowing exactly what use to put him
to.   At last a hirer came, and a bright day for Lessing
and for Germany seemed at last to have dawned.   Herr
Löwen, a dramatic poet and critic in Hamburg, had
published a volume of "Theatrical Writings," in which
the way of reform for the German stage was marked out
with much penetration and force.   No more wandering
troupes, under the direction of an actor with axes of his
own to grind, but fixed theatres in the great towns, supported by the State, and directed by an official possessed
of adequate culture and information, but who should not
be an actor himself—this was, in Löwen's judgment, the
great need of the times ; and he demanded also the establishment of theatrical academies in which rising talent
might be wisely trained, and the encouragement of original German authorship.   Löwen's ideas have since been
largely carried out in Germany, and with noble results,
but the times were not ripe for them then.   However,
there seemed some chance that, to some limited extent,
they could be introduced with success in his own day
and in his own city.   Not, indeed, that a State Theatre
could be thought of there—but an opportunity arose for
acquiring, on easy terms, the lease of an excellent theatre
lately built in Hamburg by the actor and manager
Ackermann, whose enterprise had fallen to pieces owing
to dissensions among his company.   Twelve Hamburg

merchants accordingly formed themselves, under Löwen's influence, into a company for this purpose; appointed Löwen as general director, engaged all they could of the best acting talent in Germany (including Eckhof, "the German Garrick"), and finally offered Lessing the post of theatrical critic and general adviser, at a yearly salary of eight hundred thalers (*heavy* thalers—£160—which was not bad in times when a man could dine for 1½d.). If he would write plays too, so much the better, but no stipulation of this kind was insisted upon. His most defined duties were to write a review of each performance, criticizing both the play and the acting, in a theatrical journal to be published twice a week by the proprietors of the theatre. This journal, it was hoped, would have the threefold effect of helping the actors to an intelligent and cultivated understanding of their parts, of raising the general level of dramatic authorship in Germany, and of educating the theatre-going public to appreciate these improvements.

Lessing could have found no more congenial situation, and he accepted it with little delay, refusing for it the Professorship of Archæology at Cassel, of which his "Laocoon" had procured him the offer.

Another enterprise connected itself with the theatrical one. There was in Hamburg a man of letters named Bode, who had edited the well-known journal, *The Hamburg Correspondent*, — a capable, cultured, and honourable man, whom Lessing had met in the winter of 1766, during a visit to Hamburg, which he had made in order to look into the circumstances of the theatre there. Bode had determined to found a publishing and printing business in Hamburg, and, when Lessing accepted the offer of the National Theatre Company, invited him to take part in it. Lessing was much struck with the idea, and, after some consideration, accepted it. He had a number of friends among the most eminent writers of the day, who would give him their support; his own works, he hoped, could be published to more profit in his own office than elsewhere; and the theatre would give him and his partner all its printing, including the theatrical review which Lessing was to write.

It now remained but to shake off his load of debt, collect the sum which he had to put into the publishing enterprise, and take up his new duties. The debts amounted to over five hundred thalers, and in answer to his father's piteous appeal, he had had to send him two hundred thalers at Christmas—the goods of the poor Pastor being laid under arrest by his creditors.

Gleim—"Father Gleim,"—the good genius of many a struggling young author, knew his friend's need and sent him a timely present :—

" Why, dearest friend," he wrote, " why did you send me back the fifty thalers? [lent to Lessing on his return from his Pyrmont journey, when he paid Gleim a visit.] You should not have been in such a hurry, for I had to pay you the 10 louis d'or, which you receive herewith ; and so we could have deducted them. Only do not ask why you receive these 10 louis d'or from me ; for you will not learn it till I see you again. Meantime do not trouble yourself about it—they are absolutely your own property."

But this did not go far, and Lessing found himself compelled to sell the splendid library which he had collected while at Breslau. A sad thing indeed that such a workman should have to sell his tools; but there was no help for it. Unhappily some of his rarest acquisitions were missing, a rascally servant whom he had sent in charge of them from Breslau to Berlin having purloined them; and in Berlin, where, as he remarked, people did not know the value of such things, the remainder fetched far less than he had paid for them. Doubtless his book-buying had not been carried out on very sound commercial principles. Once, it is recorded, he had told Nicolai to attend a certain auction, and purchase a certain lot of books whatever it might cost. He had forgotten, however, that he had given exactly the same directions to another friend; and the books had risen to an astonishing price before the bewildered bidders sought an explanation from each other.

One way or another his affairs were set in such order as was possible, and in April, 1767, we find him established in Hamburg. On the 22nd the National Theatre was opened, and on the 1st day of May appeared the first number of the famous periodical known as the *Hamburgische Dramaturgie.*

It was at first intended that the players as well as the authors should be criticized, but this soon proved to be out of the question. One lady, an admirable actress too, had only taken service under the strict stipulation that she was never to be mentioned by Herr Lessing; and his first few gentle remarks on the performers whom he was permitted to criticize occasioned commotions which would speedily have wrecked the enterprise. Lessing's criticism, when he wrote in anger or contempt, was like a whip of wires. The players were safe, if they had known it, for they were weak and could not retaliate. But they did not know it, and were rejoiced to find that, after the fourth week, their education was in future to form no part of Lessing's plan.

For two years the *Hamburgische Dramaturgie* continued to appear, and in its hundred numbers Lessing's whole theory of the drama was unfolded in the very manner which suited him best—through the criticism of concrete examples of the art with which he dealt.   There was no sort of orderly sequence in the work, taken as a whole ; it simply kept pace with the performances of the theatre.   But it tried each drama in accordance with fixed and coherent principles, well thought out in Lessing's mind before he began to write.   His central objects were to exhibit the true theory of the drama as fixed by Aristotle—to show how the French school, in its supposed rigid adherence to Greek canons, had utterly misapprehended and misapplied them—to hold up Shakspere, who knew nothing of these canons, as the true heir of the greatness of the Greeks, and to inspire the German drama with a bold and native spirit, which should give it a place in its own right beside those of Greece and England.   The Greek drama had been supposed to obey those unities of time and place, the slavish adherence to which had led to so many absurdities on the French stage.   Lessing shows that it is simply the existence of the chorus in the Greek drama which prescribes these unities : if the action has to be witnessed throughout by a body of persons who cannot be supposed to go to any great distance from their own homes, or to assemble on more than one occasion, it is clear that it must transact itself in one day and on one spot.   Abolish the chorus, and where is the necessity for those unities which the French, proud of wearing as fetters the laws which with the Greeks arose from an inward necessity, endeavoured to force upon Europe as fundamental laws of the drama?   Even the Greeks, Lessing might have remarked, did not observe these laws where the inward necessity ceased to exist.   In the " Eumenides " of Æschylus, the chorus of Furies is represented as chasing Orestes about from place to place, the action lasting over several days, and the scene shifting from Delphi to Athens.[1]   The constraint of the unities of time and place was however, he observes, so turned to account by the genius of the Greeks that they won by it far oftener than they lost.   It led them of necessity to intensify passion, to banish all digression and accident, and thus to guard the one true and essential unity which the drama is everywhere bound to observe—the unity of action.

The drama, Lessing considered, can go no step outside the laws laid down by Aristotle without going wrong. What then are these laws?   That of the unity of action is the chief—the fable must be coherent, its parts duly subordinated, and each making for an end common to all. Again, characters in the drama must be types, not individuals—the spectator loses sympathy if he feels that the action is influenced by idiosyncrasies.   Neither a perfectly innocent nor a perfectly evil character must be made

---

[1] It is singular that this striking corroboration of his view was not noticed by Lessing.   But Æschylus was then little read, and less appreciated.

the victim of a tragic fate—in the one case the moral sense is wounded, in the other the sympathetic emotions, which it is the motive of tragedy to excite, are not awakened. Lessing considers at great length, in dealing with Weisse's play of Richard III., the famous passage in which Aristotle has laid it down as the aim of Tragedy to " effect, by pity and fear, the purifying of such passions." [1] He brought to bear on this obscure passage a most fruitful principle of interpretation. Aristotle, he argued, must everywhere be interpreted by himself—let us not suppose that we can be sure of his meaning in the Poetics until we have searched for light upon it from the Rhetoric and the Ethics. In the first place Corneille, and other writers, had erred in translating the word φόβος, Fear, as if it meant Terror (Schrecken).[2] The latter is a passion, rather of the nerves than of the spirit, into which we may be surprised by the spectacle of some atrocious savagery or wickedness. But Fear, φόβος, is elsewhere stated by Aristotle to be felt only in witnessing the calamities of men of the same order as ourselves (Poetics, xiii). And, again, Aristotle declares that a true tragic fable should inspire φόβος by the mere narration, without any spectacle at all. It is clear, then, that by φόβος Aristotle meant to denote a feeling which has more of the nature of sympathy with the sufferer than of terror at the tragic deed. And it is easy to see to what extravagances of revolting conception Corneille's false

---

[1] δι' ἐλέου καὶ φόβου περαίνουσα τὴν τῶν τοιούτων παθημάτων κάθαρσιν.—Poetics, vi.

[2] Lessing himself had translated it "Schrecken" in the first number of his *Theatrical Library*.

rendering of the words of Aristotle must give rise. It did, in fact, give rise to them in the works of Corneille himself, and for this reason Lessing denies him the title of the Great, and proposes to substitute that of the Monstrous or the Gigantesque.

Again, pity and fear are to effect the purifying—of what? Of all the passions of man, of his whole emotional nature, says Corneille. We are to be taught by tragic examples to shun excessive or evil passions. But this is not what Aristotle says. Pity and fear are to purify passions akin to themselves. And what is the meaning of this purification? It is something which must be effected, not by a didactic example, but by a moral influence. According to Aristotle, virtue lies in a mean between two extremes. The κάθαρσις he speaks of means the transformation of the untrained passions of pity and fear into virtuous dispositions. And this is plainly effected when he who feels too little of these emotions is made to feel more, and he who feels too much is made to feel less. It may be added that it is also a purifying of the passions when they are rightly directed ; when we are led to pity what is truly pitiable, to fear what it truly behoves us to fear.

Lessing agrees with the popular view so far as it attributes an ethical sense, that of purification, *Reinigung,* to κάθαρσις. But this is not the only sense it may have. It may mean the *purging away,* not of unwholesome elements *from* the passions, but of the very passions themselves. The dramatist is first to excite them in the mind of the spectator, then to tranquillize and subdue them. In this view Aristotle would be regarded as describing simply the effect of the drama on the feelings of the spectator while he sat in the theatre—not any permanent influence on his moral character.   And for this view there is a great deal to be said.   It is admirably illustrated by the greatest and most complete tragic work which has reached us from antiquity—the "Oresteia" of Æschylus.   Never was a dramatic action more filled with motives of pity and fear, crime breeding crime, and vengeance vengeance while innocence and righteousness seem hopelessly entangled in the fatal sequence.   Yet at the close of the trilogy we see the deluge of guilt and woe gradually sink away, the sun breaks out again, the firm, habitable land of a sound social order where men can live and work in peace begins to appear, and the Furies, mysterious and hideous instruments of divine wrath, become the protecting deities of a redeemed world. And there are even subtler ways in which the same end may be reached.   The conclusion of a drama may be as calamitous as it is possible to conceive, and yet the emotions of pity and fear may be counterbalanced by others which arise in the course of the tragic action. What can be more calamitous than the fate of the Antigone of Sophocles, of the Cordelia of Shakspere? Yet Cordelia and Antigone were true to themselves, to their own beautiful natures.   In this lies a spiritual victory which subdues our sense of their visible overthrow.

This view of Aristotle's meaning, which is substantially Goethe's, did not occur to Lessing.   If it had done so he would probably have considered it, and with justice, a less natural interpretation of Aristotle's language than his own.   But it is certainly a possible one, and one which expresses admirably the actual character of the greatest works of the ancient and modern drama.

Even at the date of the *Hamburgische Dramaturgie* Lessing had to complain of the rise of a school which, because he had exploded the French rules of dramatic art, thought it might be as lawless and capricious as it pleased. No greater mistake could have been made from Lessing's point of view. Genius may disregard existing laws, if it perceives a higher end which may be thus attained. But we shall question it rigorously as to whether it has any such end; we shall demand that, in disobeying laws heretofore approved, it shall embody and suggest deeper ones. A series of vividly conceived situations is not necessarily a drama; and herein lies the condemnation of such plays as " Götz von Berlichingen," which, on its publication some four years afterwards, Lessing seriously thought of attacking as a typical example of the errors of the new school.

It would be impossible within our limits to give anything like an adequate account of the wonderful body of criticisms collected in the *Hamburgische Dramaturgie.* Let us be content, then, with having briefly indicated something of their spirit, and proceed with our narrative.

Lessing had not been long in Hamburg before he discovered that the theatrical undertaking was doomed to failure. "No one knows," he wrote to his brother Karl, " who is cook and who is waiter." There were too many masters in the enterprise. Löwen soon gave it up, the players squabbled and mutinied, and, most fatal circumstance of all, the audiences, even in cultured and wealthy Hamburg, showed little inclination to encourage native

talent or elevated art. Nor even when buffoons and
gymnasts were called in did the vitality of the National
Theatre improve ; and its struggles ended in November
1768, when Ackermann agreed to accept the surrender
of the lease.

The *Dramaturgie*, though dated as if it had appeared
regularly twice a week up to April 25, 1768, had really
run a very fitful course after the first couple of months.
The two complete volumes were not published till April,
1769. This literary enterprise was no more successful,
from a commercial point of view, than the theatrical
one. It was true that the public bought the *Dramaturgie* eagerly enough, but they bought it in the pirated
editions which were the curse of authorship in that day,
and Lessing and his partner were not businesslike enough
to provide that the market should be at least as well
stocked with the true as with the pirated edition.
Lessing's savings melted away, and his income from the
theatre was not likely to be regularly paid when the
ticket-office used to be besieged with creditors before
every performance. He was again the " bird upon the
roof," and again the instinct to bend his flight to the
South grew strong within him.

In April, 1768, he visited Leipzig for the great Easter
Fair, where he had business connected with his publishing enterprise to transact. Goethe was then a student
at the university there, and might have met Lessing if he
had chosen ; but some caprice which he never ceased to
regret kept him from doing so.

On his way back from Leipzig, Lessing had intended
to pay a visit to Halle in order to see Professor Klotz, a

scholar, or quasi-scholar, of great eminence there, who had hailed the " Laocoon " with enthusiastic praise in a literary journal which he edited. Circumstances, however, led him to change his mind, and instead of a friendly visit from Lessing, Klotz found himself treated to a polemic, for the ruthless severity of which there are few parallels in literature. Klotz was a writer of much elegance, but of shallow learning and insincere character. His accomplishments, backed by skilful intriguing, had won him Frederick's favour, and a handsome salary ; and he soon began to form a coterie of flatterers and followers whose praises should swell his hollow reputation, and whose tongues he could turn, like a bravo's dagger, against any dangerous competitor. On the publication of the "Laocoon," he had endeavoured to enlist Lessing under his flag, and Lessing replied politely to his effusive correspondence. But Lessing discovered in time the falseness of his pretensions to learning, and the unworthy arts with which he backed them, and quietly let the connection drop. Klotz saw what this meant. If a writer of Lessing's force could not be won he must be discredited, and the first step to this was a catalogue of errors supposed to be contained in the " Laocoon," which Klotz put forward in a work on engraved gems in classical times. Klotz's reviewers took the cue—one of them exulted in the discovery, in the "Laocoon," of at least one "unpardonable" error, and Lessing resolved to expose Klotz and his clique in a way which would not soon be forgotten. The works in which this aim was carried out are three in number : a treatise on " The Ancestral Portraits of the Romans," an essay entitled

" How the Ancients Represented Death," and a series
of " Antiquarian Letters." In the latter Lessing began
by showing that Klotz's criticisms on the " Laocoon "
proved nothing except his own unpardonable haste and
ignorance. He had culpably misread the author whom
he pretended to correct, and committed himself to
obvious absurdities in the attempt to confute him. Then
Lessing invaded the enemy's country. He battered
stronghold after stronghold about his ears. He showed
that his learning was borrowed, and that he misunderstood what he borrowed. He laid bare the base arts by
which Klotz had sought to swell his own reputation and
blast that of other men. Never was an exposure more
searching and scathing—never before had Lessing wielded
his marvellous style with such passion and power. Indeed the *casus belli* looks petty enough when compared
with the onslaught which it brought about. " Klotz
threw a pea at Lessing," said one, " and Lessing replied
with an avalanche of rocks." This is true, but it is not
the whole truth. Klotz was becoming a public nuisance
and the bane of learning with his pea-shooter. Poisoned
darts sometimes flew from it too. The weal of the
republic of letters demanded his extinction.

Klotz made little attempt to defend himself, con-
tenting himself mainly by publishing in the journals he
edited insinuations about Lessing and the Hamburg
actresses ; and died while the controversy was in progress.

The " Antiquarian Letters " were followed by the little
treatise on the representation of Death among the
ancients, which grew out of a comment of Klotz on a

note in the " Laocoon." In all Lessing's writings there is nothing finer in style and thought than this tract. Count Caylus, an antiquarian writer with whom the " Laocoon " is much concerned, had suggested as a subject for pictorial representation the passage in the Iliad in which the body of Sarpedon was delivered to Sleep and Death ; expressing, however, his doubt as to whether the figure of Sleep, with its attributes, could be artistically harmonized with the hideous skeleton which he assumed, as all then did, to have been the usual representation of Death among the ancients. Lessing argues from a number of sculptures, which he was the first to interpret correctly, that this view of the representation of Death was wholly mistaken. The ancients pictured Death under no horrible aspect, but as the beautiful twin-brother of Sleep—a Genius leaning on a reversed torch, and often accompanied by a butterfly, the emblem of the soul. Skeletons certainly were sculptured in antiquity, but they, as Lessing judges from a passage of Seneca (Epist. xxiv.), were the *larvæ* or ghosts of wicked men condemned to haunt the earth, and never a representation of the general conception of Death. The effect of this little treatise was immediate and profound. It was an authentic ray from Hellas, and before it the foul apparitions which had symbolized death vanished from art, and images of calm and beauty took their place.

The hopes for the reformation of the stage which Lessing had cherished when he decided to go to Hamburg, seemed, before he left that city, destined to be fulfilled in a very unexpected way. Klopstock,

who was at this time living at Hamburg, and whom
Lessing constantly met, had attracted the attention of
the Emperor Joseph II., Frederick's too impatient disciple, who also aimed at making his royalty a "glorious
servitude," and who was especially anxious to encourage
native German literature in his dominions.   Under
Klopstock's influence a beautiful scheme was framed
by which an academy was to be founded at Vienna,
and the State Theatre there reformed, with Lessing
as one of its directors.   Lessing was much impressed
with the proposal, although Nicolai warned him against
accepting it.   How, asked Nicolai, could he find
himself at home under a Catholic despotism, in a city
where Mendelssohn's noble dialogue on the immortality
of the soul had lately been confiscated? As good
Prussians, Gleim, Nicolai, and the rest of Lessing's
friends, were inclined to think Vienna a very poor ex-
change for Berlin.   But Lessing had contracted a deep,
and partly just, dislike for the Prussian capital, which
Frederick's stupid treatment of him had not tended to
soften.

"The colony of learned men," [the proposed Academy at Vienna]
he wrote to Nicolai in August, 1769, "which seems to you so
ridiculous, is, in my judgment, not so ridiculous at all. Nor will they
want for liberty to think in Vienna. And where can a learned
man be deprived of this liberty? But a fool must *write* everything
he thinks. . . ."

And a few days later :—

. . . "Vienna may be what it will ; yet I would promise better
fortune for German literature there than in your Frenchified Berlin.
If the " Phædon " has been confiscated in Vienna, it must have only

happened because it was printed in Berlin, and no one could imagine that any one in Berlin would *defend* the immortality of the soul. And do not talk to me of your Berlin freedom of thinking and writing. It amounts simply and solely to the freedom of publishing as many *sottises* against religion as one likes. And of this freedom a good man must soon be ashamed to make use. But let any one try in Berlin to write as freely about other things as Sonnenfels has done in Vienna; let him try to tell the truth to the genteel rabble at Court as he has done; let some one come forward in Berlin and raise his voice for the rights of the subject, and against extortion and despotism, as is done now even in France and Denmark, and you will soon find out which country is to the present day the most enslaved in Europe."

This is exaggerated. During the Seven Years' War, Lessing used to get himself into trouble in Saxony by defending the Prussians, and in Berlin, as Nicolai tells us, by doing the same for the Austrians: he was a great enemy of human self-complacency. However, the Vienna project came to nothing, and Lessing was still to hire, although it appears that, if he had chosen to forego his Italian journey, he might have had an engagement as dramatic author at the Vienna theatre with a good salary. But where were the means for the Italian journey to come from? "My heart bleeds," he wrote to Karl, "to think of our parents. But God is my witness that it is not for want of will that I do not give them full assistance. I am at this moment certainly the poorest of our whole family; for the poorest of them at least owes nothing," [thanks to him]—"and I, in order to procure the most necessary things, am often up to the ears in debt. God help us!"

Rescue did come in time. Among the friends Lessing had made in Hamburg was one Johann Arnold Ebert,

9

a native of that city, who, at the time when Lessing knew him, was professor at the "Collegium Carolinum" in Brunswick. The two men had many literary sympathies in common, especially the love of English literature, and Ebert, dreading that if something were not done for Lessing he might be lost to Germany, persuaded the Crown Prince, and *de facto* ruler of Brunswick, to offer him the post of Librarian at the Wolfenbüttel Library. After a personal interview (Nov., 1769), in which Lessing fancied, quite mistakenly, that his independent bearing had prejudiced the Prince against him, the arrangement was concluded, on the understanding that Lessing was shortly to have leave of absence for his Italian journey; and he promised to enter upon his new duties in about two months.

His residence at Hamburg, in spite of his disappointments, had been a pleasant and profitable one. The social atmosphere of the flourishing Free Town, in which there was much of true culture, and less of buckram and constraint than in Berlin, had suited him exactly, and he had made many friends there. In the circle of the family of Hermann Samuel Reimarus, Professor of Oriental Languages at the gymnasium in Hamburg, he was a particularly welcome guest. He was also on friendly terms with Goeze, the pastor of St. Katherine's Church, and their intimacy caused not a little wonder and disgust among Lessing's friends. These were mostly either freethinkers, or at least friends of the new "rationalistic" school of theology, and Goeze was as vehement and narrow a champion of the old Lutheran orthodoxy as Lessing's own father, whose hatred of the stage he also shared, although he explicitly excepted the plays of Lessing from his general condemnation. Another Hamburg friend of Lessing's was one Samuel König, a silk manufacturer. His wife, Eva König, was then a woman of some thirty-five years of age—vivacious, cultured, and feminine, with a face expressing much sweetness and strength of character, not without a gleam of wholesome satire. With her, her husband, and their four children, Lessing became very intimate, and on the death of König, while on a journey to Venice, in 1769, Lessing, in accordance with a wish which his friend had expressed as they parted, took charge of the affairs of his family. These were found to be in a very critical and complicated state; and it is perhaps owing to this circumstance, perhaps also in some degree to the tender feeling with which he was beginning to regard Eva König, that his departure for Wolfenbüttel was delayed till long after the appointed time. At last, however, in April, 1770, he arrived on the scene of his new duties, and was formally installed in the office which he held till his death. He was a "bird on the roof" no longer— unhappily he was to feel too often that a bird on the roof is better off than a bird in a cage.

CHAPTER XII

THE Library of Wolfenbüttel, or "Bibliotheca Augusta," had been founded in the seventeenth century by Augustus, Duke of Brunswick, Wolfenbüttel being the capital of the Duchy. It contained an admirable collection of books, and was especially rich in editions of the Bible. Its collection of manuscripts, too, was thought to be a very valuable one; and, as we shall see, there were treasures in this department which it was left for Lessing to bring to light. He was at first delighted with his position. He had leisure ("they wish the library to be of use to me rather than me to it"), and a salary of six hundred thalers a year, with lodging and fuel. He had also received from the Duke the valuable privilege of freedom of the censorship for works published through the ducal printing-office. Wolfenbüttel itself had the gloom of a deserted capital—the reigning Duke having transferred his residence to Brunswick—and this, to a man of Lessing's nature and habits, was a serious drawback to his contentment. But Brunswick was only some seven miles distant, and in Brunswick the Hereditary Prince had assembled a circle of able and learned men about him, just as his nephew, Karl August of

Weimar, afterwards did at the latter Court. The Prince himself was a man of very remarkable character and accomplishments—a general who had won the warm praise of his uncle Frederick, a student of literature, and a musician and actor of great talent. Besides Ebert, Lessing found in Brunswick the poets Zachariä and Gärtner, the theologian Schmidt, the Abbot Jerusalem of Riddinghausen,[1] Eschenburg, an author with whom Lessing soon became closely intimate, and others. The Prince had even sought out Mendelssohn at Berlin, and endeavoured to win him for Brunswick—a proof of liberality and insight with which Lessing was naturally much pleased.

As soon as Lessing had settled himself in Wolfenbüttel he began to explore the treasures under his control, and was not long in discovering among them a jewel of much value. It lay hid in a collection of MSS. which had belonged to the Abbey of Weissenburg in Elsass, and had been purchased in the previous century for the Wolfenbüttel Library when on the point of being sold for old parchment to the goldbeaters of Frankfurt. It was an answer by Berengarius of Tours, the famous liberal theologian of the eleventh century, to the attack made by Lanfranc, Archbishop of Canterbury, on his doctrine of the Eucharist. The very existence of such an answer had been unknown—the "recreant Berengare," who, in rejecting the doctrine of Transubstantiation, had incurred the hostility of the great body of the clergy of

---

[1] Father of the Jerusalem whose suicide suggested "Werther" to Goethe. He was a Protestant, nothing remaining of the Abbacy except its title and its revenue.

his day, had, it was thought, been converted by his formidable opponent. Lessing's discovery makes it clear that this precursor of the Reformation died as he had lived, and throws much new light on the Eucharistic controversies of his day. When, however, Lessing urged that the true teaching of Berengarius was almost precisely that of Luther, he was, in the judgment of all the best authorities, mistaken. It was Calvin's doctrine— one still further removed from that of Rome—and not Luther's, that Berengarius had anticipated.

Lessing at first intended to publish the MS. with an introduction, but he ultimately decided to leave this task to some future hand,[1] renouncing his rights of first discovery, and to write a historical treatise on the subject instead.

This occupied him during the summer of 1770. When the treatise appeared, in the autumn of that year, it was recognized at once as entirely worthy of its author, little as any one had expected to see him labouring in such a field. The great Biblical critic, Ernesti of Leipzig, pointed to it as a proof of his favourite maxim that a scholar thoroughly versed in the *humaniora* is capable of treating any subject to good purpose.

Lessing's apparent defence of the Lutheran doctrine of the Eucharist was the cause of much perturbation to the rising Rationalistic school, led by Professor Semler of Halle, whose object was to reconcile a respect for the text of the Scriptures with the utmost possible elimination of every mystical and supernatural element. Lessing's

---

[1] It was published in Berlin, 1834, but (say Guhrauer and others) in a very unscholarly fashion.

detestation of this school was very deep, and equally deep was its disgust and perplexity at being detested by him. Was he not himself known to hold the most liberal, not to say sceptical views upon the fundamental dogmas of Christianity? It was true; but he held exceedingly strict views upon the obligations of veracity and logic; and he considered these obligations outraged by the attempt to "rationalize" doctrines which, whether revealed by God or invented by man, had never appealed to the judgment of common sense. His dislike of Rationalism was simply an instance of that hatred of the confusion of things naturally distinct and separate which had led him, in the "Laocoon," to make war on allegorical painting and descriptive poetry.

"With orthodoxy," he wrote to Karl, in 1774, "one knew pretty well what to be at : between it and philosophy a partition-wall had been erected, behind which each could go its own way without hindering the other. But what is being done now? They tear down this partition-wall, and, under the pretext of making us rational Christians, they make us most irrational philosophers. I beg you, my dear brother, inquire more closely into this point, and look less at what our new theologians fling away than at what they wish to put in its place. We are agreed that our old religious system is false ; but I should not like to say with you that it is a patchwork of bunglers and half-philosophers. I know of nothing in the world in which the acuteness of the human intellect has been more exhibited and exercised than in this. The patchwork of bunglers and half-philosophers is the religious system which they now want to set in the place of the old, and that with much more influence on reason and philosophy than the ancient system ever claimed. And yet you take it ill of me that I defend this ancient system !"

Unhappily by the time that Lessing's treatise on Berengarius was published, one, who he hoped would

have read it with more than common pleasure, was no
more. The old Pastor, whose last days had been
darkened by want and care and the enmity of his own
flock, died in August, 1770, sorely lamented by Lessing. He at once made himself responsible for his
father's debts, and did what he could to help and comfort
his mother and sister. He meditated writing some
account of his father, "which should be read longer than
six months, and in other places than Kamenz," but the
plan was never carried out.

A valuable authority on Lessing's inward and outward
life in Wolfenbüttel for the next five or six years is his
correspondence with Eva König, the widow of his Hamburg friend. They were betrothed to each other—the
fact being kept strictly secret from the world—during a
short visit which he paid to Hamburg in the autumn of
1771. Except for his passing attachment to the actress
Lorenz, in Leipzig, Lessing had, up to his present mature
age, been curiously free from the influence of the other
sex. Neither in his life nor in his art was there a trace
of it. Women in his lyrics are objects of gallantry or of
satire, never of romantic passion. His affection for Eva
König is probably not to be called romantic either, but it
was as warm and deep as any woman could desire. Unhappily her late husband's affairs turned out to have been
left in a very unsatisfactory condition, and with Lessing's
small income, which was not enough for himself, there
could be no possibility of their marrying until she had
disposed of the business she had inherited, which,
owing to want of capital, she could not manage to any

good purpose. It was several years before this could be effected—years in which the lovers had much to endure besides the mere postponement of their union.

Lessing's early volume of lyrics and epigrams continued to be sought for by the public, although he himself had reached a stage from which he could look at it only with distaste. No one could have judged his work more severely than he did himself. In heartily condemning some of Karl's plays, he adds that he thinks them quite as good as his own first pieces. There is a famous passage in the *Hamburgische Dramaturgie* in which he renounces all claim to poetic genius, attributing his successes in the drama to study and the critical faculty alone. Now he thought the trouble of supervising a new edition of his early works, which the publisher Voss found himself obliged by threat of piracy to bring out, more than the "rubbish" was worth. He handed the poems over to Ramler, begging him to revise and amend them as best he could, and to let him see no more of them. The volume appeared in 1771. In order that the public might get some grain amid all this chaff, Lessing enriched it with the fine treatise on the epigram of which mention has been already made.

In the same year Lessing had promised Voss to prepare an edition of his dramatic works, with a new piece, to be named " Emilia Galotti." As we know, it had been long ago begun in Leipzig, at the rate of " seven lines in seven days"; and now, in spite of the disgust with all theatrical affairs with which the Hamburg fiasco had filled him, he took it up again. The actor Döbbelin, manager of the theatre in Brunswick, having got wind of this new play, begged Lessing to have it ready for representation on the birthday of the Duchess, March 13, 1772 ; and he consented. But he had forgotten to take into account his own fastidious and dilatory methods of work, and although the play was ready in time (barely in time to let the actors study their parts), it was finished under conditions of haste and vexation by no means favourable to artistic production. "The nearer I come to the end," he wrote to Voss, on January 25th, "the less it pleases me."

In "Emilia Galotti" Lessing transferred to modern days, and divested of all "Staatsinteresse" or political interest, the antique theme which he had already attempted to treat in dramatic form—the story of the Roman Virginia, whom her father slays to save her from the dishonour with which she is threatened by an infamous ruler. Lessing's "Virginia" was, however, inspired by the "Julius Cæsar" of Shakspere, while "Emilia" certainly springs from the same artistic impulse which produced "Miss Sara Sampson." It is a *tragédie bourgeoise*. Nor does it only resemble the latter play by falling within the same class. In each play we have a heroine whose greatest danger is her own weakness. Sara has yielded to seduction ; Emilia dies because she fears to do so. In each play the seducer is a man rather thoughtless and pleasure-loving than actively wicked. And in each the catastrophe is brought about by a jealous and passionate woman, in depicting whose fierce energy Lessing has spent his utmost art. But to compare the merits of the two plays as works of art would be preposterous. "Sara" is often weak, incoherent, tedious; " Emilia " is all fire and force, and shows, too, a power of subtle characterization for which we have scarcely been prepared by any previous work of Lessing's. The Prince's character is a particularly fine example of this subtlety of conception—a man with many engaging qualities—love of art, refined sentiment, quick impressionability ; yet at bottom utterly worthless, and capable of sacrificing anything rather than the least of his caprices. Odoardo, too, the father of Emilia, with his sternness, rectitude, and fiery energy, is an admirably conceived character, and so is the worldly and foolish mother. Of Emilia herself it is, however, difficult to form any consistent view. In the beginning of the play she is a very Desdemona in her childlike innocence of heart. Towards the end, after her bridegroom has been murdered almost before her eyes, she entreats her father to slay her—why? Not because she has violence to fear at the hands of the Prince to whose castle she has been borne, with what designs she well knows, but because she has doubts of her own steadfastness. Odoardo has shown her a dagger, given him by Orsina, the Prince's deserted mistress, with which he had meant to kill her would-be seducer.

Emilia. No, for heaven's sake, my father !—This life is all the vicious have. Me, me, father ! give me this dagger.
Odoardo. Child, it is no hairpin.
Emilia. Then let hairpins be daggers. It is all one.
Odoardo. What? Is it come to that ? No, no ! Bethink thee. Thou too hast but one life to lose.
Emilia. And but one innocence.
Odoardo. Which is beyond all force.

Emilia. But not beyond all temptation.   Force ! Force ! who cannot
defy force ?   What force does is nothing : temptation is
the true force.—I have blood, my father, as young and
warm as any.   And my senses, too, are senses.   I
stand for nothing.   I am good for nothing. . . . Give
me, my father, give me this dagger.

Odoardo. And if you knew it—this dagger.

Emilia. And if I know it not ?—An unknown friend is still a
friend.   Give it me, my father, give it me !

Odoardo. Shall I now give it to thee ?—There !   [*gives the dagger.*]

Emilia. And there !   [*as she is about to pierce herself with it, the
father tears it again out of her hand.*]

Odoardo. See—how hasty !—Nay, that is not for thy hand.

Emilia. True ; I must do it with a hairpin [*she puts up her hand to
seek for one, and touches a rose in her hair*].   Thou
here still ?—Down with thee ! thou art not for the hair
of one—such as my father will have me !

Odoardo. O my daughter !—

Emilia. O my father, did I guess right ?   Yet, no—you would not
have that.   Why did you then delay ? [*in a bitter tone,
as she plucks the rose to pieces.*]   Long ago, indeed, there
was a father who, to save his daughter's honour, seized
the nearest blade his hand could find, and drove it to
her heart—gave her life a second time.   But all such
deeds are of long ago.   There are no such fathers
now !

Odoardo. There are, my daughter, there are !   [*stabbing her*]   God !
what have I done ? [*she sinks down and he holds her in
his arms.*]

Emilia. Plucked a rose, before the storm had stripped it of its
leaves.   Let me kiss it, this fatherly hand.

Every sentence in this scene throbs with such concentrated passion that one can hardly criticize it coldly.
But, as Lessing himself has said, it is against the master
that the critic must be most carefully on his guard.   And
if we compel ourselves to assume this critical attitude, we

must confess that Lessing has supplied no adequate and natural motive for the terrible act of Odoardo. Nor is it in the interests of a crude poetic justice that we demand to see some punishment inflicted on the Prince and his more wicked counsellor, Marinelli. Lessing himself has urged that a drama must not be a fragment of life, but an image of it; and a true image of life must indicate that moral order which Lessing certainly believed to be perceptible in it when looked at as a whole.

But, with whatever faults, the play remains a noble and powerful work. Lessing does not, as he had at first intended, use " all the liberties of the English stage," but he profits, as he found the Greeks did, by the constraint of the unities, in letting them intensify the passion and concentrate the interest of the piece. It has an athletic severity of outline—there is not a speech in it that has not its dramatic use, and the style is close and concentrated almost to a fault. It is true that all the personages talk like Lessing—but who would not hear Lessing talk ?

" Emilia Galotti " was performed with great success in Brunswick, and was soon added to the *répertoire* of nearly every German company. The Hereditary Prince was present at the performance, and followed it attentively; but the Court is said to have taken no notice of the author upon the production, in honour of the ducal family, of the greatest German tragedy. Possibly the Duke, and his courtiers and mistresses, winced at more than one touch in Lessing's description of the Court of Guastella. Lessing certainly had it in his mind to castigate the abominable tyrannies and vices of some of the petty

German princes, in the dominions of one of whom, at least (Gotha), the play was forbidden to be acted.

In 1773 Lessing began to publish those "Contributions to History and Literature from the Treasures of the Wolfenbüttel Library," which the contents of some of the later issues made so famous. Unknown MSS. and *notabilia* of all kinds are included in these papers, which he issued through the ducal printing-office at irregular intervals, according as he found material. Often his own commentary or introduction adds high value to these " Contributions " ; and the variety of subjects which he treats with learning and insight is amazing: —the discovery of oil-painting, ancient German poetry, the Greek anthology, the Flemish Chronicle, astrology— nothing came amiss to him. Two of these papers, which brought new evidence to bear on the views of Leibnitz upon the doctrines of the Trinity and of eternal punishment, gave much offence to the Rationalists. In each case he claimed Leibnitz as a supporter of the orthodox view ; and in the paper on the Trinity he ridiculed the modern theologians who, in endeavouring to commend Christianity to the understanding, had made it far less credible than when true belief in it was looked on as unattainable except by the supernatural influence of Divine grace.

His labour at these " Contributions " became in time exceedingly distasteful to him, but it brought him a few louis d'or occasionally, it was easily done, and he had, to use a favourite expression of his, to "bore the plank where it was thinnest." His sister was urgent and inconsiderate in her demands for money, and to keep his Hamburg creditors from proceeding to extremities he had again and again to request—never in vain—large advances of his salary.

Under these circumstances he began to consider whether he had not better seek for some more lucrative employment, such as he might easily have obtained in Vienna or Dresden. The Hereditary Prince, however, got wind of his meditations, and made proposals which had the effect of retaining him at Wolfenbüttel. An official, the Hofrath Lichtenstein, had recently died (Jan. 23, 1773), whose function it had been to advise the ducal family on questions relating to its historical rights and privileges. The Prince offered Lessing this post in addition to his Librarianship, and promised that he should be well treated in the matter of salary. Lessing, however, must decide to devote his career henceforth to the service of the ducal house, and give up his plans for roaming about the world. Lessing agreed. Nothing could be done at that moment, for the Prince had to start on a journey to Berlin. He returned, and Lessing expected that matters would be at once arranged; but still nothing was done. Lessing made indirect inquiries—"No answer, or as good as none," he wrote to Eva, and his wrath began to rise. Was the Prince playing with him? Was he only dangling temptations before him to induce him not to shame Brunswick by leaving its service because it could not provide for him? For Eva's sake, and at her earnest entreaty, he refrained from throwing up his post. But life in Wolfenbüttel became hateful to him; he lost all pleasure in his

work, and could do nothing except " bore his plank where
it was thinnest " in a state of silent indignation and gloom.
At last he resolved to bring matters to a crisis, and in
January, 1775, he started on a journey of adventure to
Vienna, where he should at least have the pleasure of
seeing Eva, who had travelled thither to look after her
silk-factories.   Perhaps, he thought, if he found himself
as well received there as the Imperial Ambassador at
Berlin had assured him he would be, they might never
have to part again.

In order to obtain from the Imperial Ambassador
letters of introduction which might serve him in
Vienna, Lessing travelled first to Berlin.   Thence he
proceeded to Dresden, where he delayed to receive
formal leave of absence from Wolfenbüttel ; and he
finally reached Vienna on March 31st.   " I hope," he
wrote to Eva from his inn, " that I have arrived even
sooner than you expected.   Judge from that of my
longing to embrace you."   Since their betrothal they
had only met once, when she paid Brunswick a passing
visit on her journey to Vienna.   Her affairs had now
been arranged.   The factories were disposed of, and an
income of five or six hundred thalers secured to her and
her children.   No serious obstacle to their union seemed
to remain.

But Lessing's connection with Brunswick was to entail
on him still further and harder trials.   At Vienna he
was received (writes Gebler, a friend of Eva's) with such
respect by all classes, from the Court down to the
populace, as no German author had ever met with before.
" Emilia " was played in his honour at the State Theatre,

and on his entrance he was enthusiastically greeted by the audience. Maria Theresa received him cordially, and sought his opinion and advice on the condition of literature and learning in Vienna; on which points he could and would say nothing that was pleasant for her to hear. But no definite proposals were made to him, and he soon found himself in a painful dilemma. He had made the acquaintance, at the Court of Vienna, of the youngest Prince of the House of Brunswick, then a youth of twenty-two, who was about to proceed on a journey to Venice, pending the decision of the Duke on the question whether he should enter the Prussian or the Austrian military service. He begged Lessing to be his travelling companion to Venice; and between compliance with this request and the abandonment of his present position and future hopes in Brunswick, there was no alternative for Lessing. How much he had once longed to visit Italy, and how much he now longed to decline the opportunity! But he chose the more prudent course, and the travellers started in April, 1775.

The Prince had merely proposed a trip to Venice, but his tour was extended far beyond the original plan. Lessing was deeply vexed, but there was no help for it. "That is what comes of dealing with princes," he wrote to Eva. "One can never count on anything for certain with them; and when they have once got one in their claws, he must abide by it, whether he likes it or not."

Lessing had to abide by it for nine months instead of for the few weeks he had at first reckoned on. He saw Florence, Leghorn, Genoa, Pavia, Bologna, Rome, Naples; he conversed with Pope Pius VI., who urged him to write a description of Rome, and with learned men wherever he went; and he studied the habits and characteristics of the modern people as well as the remains of ancient art. But the journey was never turned to account in a continuation of the "Laocoon," or indeed in literary work of any kind—even his diary of the journey contains little but the barest memoranda. The conditions under which he travelled were not indeed favourable to serious study. It was the hottest time of the year, Lessing was often unwell, and he found himself compelled to attend the Prince to all kinds of frivolous festivities instead of pursuing his own objects. Worst of all, the greater part of the time was passed by him in a state of the most painful anxiety about Eva. She had left Vienna shortly after his own departure, and it had been arranged between them that their letters should be sent to a friend in Vienna who should forward them to their destination, wherever that might happen to be at the time. By some stupidity or other ["did not know well where Lessing was, &c.,"] he omitted to do so, and Lessing never heard from Eva after leaving Venice. He wrote from Florence entreating her to relieve his apprehensions, but no answer reached him, and at last he gave up writing, and dragged about with him for the rest of his journey the thought that she might be dead, or seriously ill, or changed towards him—thoughts which of course afflicted her in equal measure when his letters ceased to arrive. Disappointment and pain were all that came of the fulfilment of his long cherished hope. But what then? Man is not made to have everything his own way, and Lessing had a vital sense of this important truth. What we are made for, we can do. Lessing and his betrothed were patient and true, and did the duties which life demanded of them, until in good time the clouds of doubt and anxiety rolled away.

In December the young Prince received his appointment in the Prussian army, and at once set out for home. Lessing accompanied him as far as Munich, and thence turned to Vienna, where he found Eva's letters in the hands of Gebler and another friend, and heard what he called their "bald excuses" for the negligence which had cost him so much pain. He travelled home through Dresden, where he was told [if one could put any trust in these princes!] that if he chose to enter Saxon service he would be nobly provided for; and he spent four days with his old mother at Kamenz. He saw also his brother Theophilus, now rector of the school at Pirna, and ultimately reached Brunswick in February, 1776, after a short visit to Berlin.

He was determined to allow no further uncertainty to prevail about his position in Brunswick. The Chamberlain Kuntsch had already been commissioned, since Lessing's return from Italy, to make him new proposals. He had accepted them. He had seen the Prince, who promised to send for him speedily; and yet he was still mocked by unaccountable delays. Lessing wrote to Eva that he would give the Prince till the 3rd of March to send for him. On the 2nd he wrote :—

"If he sends for me now, he shall hear all that is in my heart; if not, he shall have on Wednesday at farthest a letter from me such as I think he has not often received."

The Prince did not send, and the letter was written,

announcing Lessing's intention of sending in his resignation, and painting so vividly the Prince's unworthy conduct towards him for the last three years, that, says Lessing, it must have touched him to the quick. Such an outburst from one of the greatest masters of human speech would have been even better worth reading than Dr. Johnson's famous letter to Lord Chesterfield, but unhappily we can judge of it only from its effect on Eva :—

"If I had not already prized and loved you as much as any one can love, your letters to the Prince would have made me do so. While reading them I embraced you in my thoughts a hundred times."

"After all," wrote Lessing of the Prince at a later time, "he has a noble nature." He did not resent Lessing's plain speaking, begged him to take no step towards his resignation for the present, and ultimately, in a personal interview, settled his position in a manner as satisfactory as the revenue of the Duchy—all that could be spared from the Duke's amusements and mistresses—would reasonably permit. Lessing was to receive an advance of one thousand thalers to pay his debts, the sum due as repayment of previous advances was to be wiped out, and his salary was to be raised by two hundred thalers. Some improvement in lodging was also arranged for; and Lessing received the title of Hofrath at the desire of the old Duke, although, as he remarks, "I told them in broad German how little I cared for that."

Now the way was clear to his marriage, but there was still some delay. He was engaged in serious literary work—likely, as he well knew, to be the most serious in worldly and visible consequences that he had ever put his hand to. This was the publication, in the Wolfenbüttel Contributions, of certain fragments of a MS. on the history of Christianity, which he had brought with him from Hamburg, the work of the late Professor Reimarus there, from whose daughter Elise he had received it. One Fragment he had published in 1774, ostensibly as a MS. of unknown authorship discovered by him in the Library. The issue of the Contributions which he was now preparing would contain nothing but five further Fragments, in which the impossibility of a rational belief in revealed religion was argued on *à priori* grounds, and the actual origin of Christianity traced to deliberate imposture. The Fragments were to be accompanied with "Gegensätze," or objections, of his own, in which the true line of defence for Christianity was indicated. Every syllable, both of attack and defence, would be read with the closest attention throughout Germany. Semler and his school, with their investigations into the origin of the canon, and their reduction of many Christian doctrines to attempts on the part of Jesus and His apostles to accommodate their teaching to local and temporary ideas, had awakened a popular interest in theological study unparalleled since the Reformation. No expenditure of time and pains in the preparation of the work on which Lessing was now engaged could be out of place.

Another work which engaged him in this year was an edition of the philosophic essays of Karl Wilhelm Jerusalem, son of the Abbot, a young man whose intellect and character and tragic end had deeply impressed Lessing. In his preface to this work he endeavoured to rescue his friend's memory from the stain cast upon it by Goethe's " Werther." Jerusalem was no morbid sentimentalist, but a strong and keen thinker in whom German philosophy endured a serious loss.

At last, in August, he visited Hamburg, and saw Eva for the first time since they had parted in Vienna. Arrangements were made for their wedding in a couple of months. His outlook in the worldly sense was bright enough just now, and was made still brighter by proposals made by the Elector Palatine, in connection with the theatre and academy at Mannheim ; although these in their ultimate issue only went with other experiences of Lessing's to inspire the bitter line in " Nathan " :—

" What is there then too little for the great ? "

In October he returned to Hamburg, and he and Eva were married on the 8th, in the house of friends named Schuback. Very few guests were present at the wedding, and everything was conducted as quietly as possible. They at once travelled to Wolfenbüttel, and took up their quarters in a small house opposite the Library; Eva having refused to occupy a much finer residence in Brunswick, because she could not visit him at his labours whenever she chose. The eldest of her family, a lad of 19, named Theodor, was then in Landau ; but the three others, Amalia, a girl of 15, Engelbert and Fritz, aged respectively 11 and 8, lived with their mother and stepfather.

CHAPTER XIII.

LESSING'S home-life is very beautiful to contemplate —a beautiful episode in his life of toil and combat. His visitors speak of Eva with enthusiasm—her "divine serenity," and the "enchanting sympathy" by which she spread its influence over all who came into her society. That she was witty, vivacious, and cultured, her letters testify—a better companion for Lessing could hardly have been found. Her serenity was sometimes tried, for Lessing had a way, the objections to which housewives will understand, of bringing home unexpected guests, visitors to the Library and so forth, to dinner. "Let us make it out with ham and eggs," he would say, if the ordinary provisions were lacking—hospitably heedless of the fact that even that dish is not a spontaneous product of the larder. The bitter and angry moods to which, for all his geniality, he was sometimes subject, grew rare; and Mendelssohn, who rejoiced the Lessings by visiting them at Wolfenbüttel, wonders to what the change can be due —"your wife? or freemasonry? [this satirical, for Lessing had lately joined the Freemasons, rather to Mendelssohn's annoyance] better reason? or riper years?" Amalia and the younger boys found in him a wise and affectionate guardian, one who joined heartily in their sports, and sought in every way to win their confidence.

Lessing's own life was quiet and regular, and, restless as he was, his wife's company made him long content with this peaceful order. He rose at six, or earlier, every morning; worked till midday, either at his own literary tasks or in performance of his official duties; dinner was at half-past twelve, and was accompanied by cheerful talk, in which he would have all take part; in the afternoon he took a walk, and found it to agree with him very well if he went as far as Brunswick. If a friend came in during the evening, he found Lessing unoccupied, and himself welcome, especially if he was a chess player.

Lessing's dress was now, as always, elegant and even fashionable. He hated dirt and confusion, and in his study, where he worked at a large oak table, with his favourite cat beside him, all was neatness and order.

The work which he produced at this time is, both in thought and in style, among the noblest, if it is not the very noblest, of his whole life. Much of the five dialogues on Freemasonry, of which the first three were published in 1778, was now written. Lessing had become a Mason, more for social than any other reasons, while on a visit to Hamburg in the autumn of 1771. A Baron von Rosenberg, who had in that year founded a lodge in Hamburg, was chiefly instrumental in winning him for the Order. Lessing does not seem to have discovered even as much as he expected in it, for on Rosenberg's remarking to him after his initiation, "You find now that we have really no designs against religion and the State," he only replied, " I wish to Heaven I had found them, for I should then at any rate have found *something*."

His further connection with the Order was of the slightest kind, yet it brought him a certain amount of annoyance. Mendelssohn, whom he saw shortly afterwards in Berlin, questioned him so closely as to the revelations which were understood to accompany initiation, that Lessing had at last to remind his friend that he was sworn to the strictest secresy. " What!" cried Mendelssohn, angrily, " have we sought Truth together for twenty years, and have you now taken an oath not to reveal to me anything you may have discovered ? " Very probably Lessing hinted to him and other inquirers that the veil of Masonic secresy hid little or nothing that was worth revealing. At any rate he called down upon himself a letter from Herr von Zinnendorf, a Mason of high rank and influence, which must have startled him not a little. He congratulates Lessing on his reception, but warns him that he has not yet been permitted to see in their full extent " the wisdom, beauty, and power " united in the institution of Masonry. It is expected of him that he shall advance its principles by playing in Brunswick the part which Socrates did among the Athenians :

" But to avoid in one form or another the unhappy fate which shortened his days, you must not step beyond the circle which Freemasonry everywhere prescribes for you ; and must ever be mindful that, even with brothers who are as well informed as ourselves, we never speak of Freemasonry, or perform the things which it enjoins on us, except behind closed doors."

He ends by demanding the surrender of a MS. on
Freemasonry which Lessing, before his entrance into the
Order, had "most improperly" intended to publish.
Here he apparently alludes to a half-jocular remark of
Lessing's to his friend Bode, that he "knew the secret of
Masonry," and meant to make it public.[1]

If Lessing was not prepared to take Freemasonry
seriously, it was clear that he had better hold himself as
much aloof from it as possible, and he chose the latter
course.   At the same time he felt that it might be a
social force of the most powerful and beneficent kind,
and he endeavoured to indicate the ideal which it might
pursue, in the dialogues entitled " Ernst und Falk." The
various lodges, he considered, bore the same relation to
Masonry in the abstract, to ideal Masonry, as the Churches
bore to the ideal Christianity ; that is to say, they had no
large or lofty conceptions of what Masonry might be and
do, and the tone of opinion which prevailed among them
was petty and mean.   Ernst, inspired by the suggestions
of his Masonic friend Falk, enters the Order in the hope
of finding there a larger and nobler life than that of the
world in which he has hitherto moved ; but he soon
finds that the brethren carry with them into the lodge
all the worldliness, frivolity, narrowness, and prejudice
which had characterized them outside of it.   He turns
to Ernst for an explanation of this great discrepancy
between the ideal and the actual, and the two friends

---

[1] There exists a first "Sketch of Ernst und Falk," certainly written
before Lessing became a Mason, and containing merely a discussion
of the historical origin of the Order.   Possibly this was the MS.
alluded to.

enter upon an animated and thoughtful discussion of the origin, the present condition, and the true functions of Freemasonry. The central idea of Falk is that the Masonic bodies are to give practical effect to the great conception of the solidarity of man—to form, in the interests of humanity at large, a counterpoise to the selfish isolating tendencies of classes and nations. The origin of the institution, in its present form and under its present name, is traced to Sir Christopher Wren, who desired to found in it a Society which should aim at the service of humanity, not, like a scientific association, by applying Truth to life, but by applying the existing forces of life to the advancement of Truth.

Lessing, it is generally thought, was entirely mistaken in his view of the historical origin of Freemasonry : Sir Christopher Wren, at least, had nothing to do with it. Nor does Masonry appear to have been much influenced by his doctrines. Indeed, in the Fourth and Fifth Dialogues he seems to suggest that the existing abuses of Masonry—its love of empty ceremonial and fantastic theory, its constant desire to put itself under the patronage of worldly rank—indicate that the world has done with it as a social force, and must seek other instruments for the realization of great humanitarian ends. These two latter dialogues were withheld from publication at the desire of Duke Ferdinand of Brunswick, a Grand Master of the Order; but they travelled about from friend to friend in MS., and were ultimately published, by whom is not known, in 1780.

" Ernst und Falk " is reckoned, and deservedly, among the very finest of Lessing's works. To find a parallel for its union of stimulating thought and exquisite literary grace, critics have with one accord turned to the Dialogues of Plato. And there is a high serenity and sweetness in it, airs from a world of pure enthusiasms and wise, calm energies, which suggest something that Shelley might have written if he had chosen rather to seek the ideal in the actual than to give actuality to the ideal.

Another work, which was largely composed during the year of Lessing's married life, stands at the very head of the religious writings which occupied his later years. This is the famous " Erziehung des Menschengeschlechts " (Education of the Human Race), a treatise consisting of a hundred short paragraphs, which contained the germ of a mighty and still unexhausted movement. To understand its significance we must realize the state of religious controversy in that day— who were the combatants and for what they contended? Three main parties are to be discerned there. Lessing found the old orthodox clergy contending for the letter of the Scriptures : every fact and every doctrine asserted in these was absolutely true in the literal sense in which it was stated ; the Bible from cover to cover was the supreme and final utterance of God's revelation to man. Against this school, but still within the limits of the Church, the Rationalists had arrayed themselves. They agreed with the orthodox in considering that the Bible contained a full and final revelation; but it contained other things too : its history was not necessarily true, even its doctrine was often to be explained as an accommodation to unenlightened local and temporary ways of thought, and Semler mocks those who think themselves the better interpreters the more of the Bible they assign to the sphere of mystery and marvel. But a residuum of absolute truth was supposed to be left, although, as Lessing indicates in a fragment of an unfinished paper on Semler, the Rationalists had no sound criterion for distinguishing between the universal and the local, the eternal and the transient. Finally, outside of the Christian body we find the Naturalists, or Deists, who held that the Scriptures were the outcome partly of designed imposture, partly of silly superstition, and that to study them, except for the sake of exposing them, was unworthy of enlightened spirits.

Not one of these three parties exists as a serious force at the present day. What are the words of those who now inherit the position of the orthodox party? "Just as no miracle has saved the texts of the Scriptures from corruption in secondary points, so no miracle has been wrought to exclude the ordinary variations of truthful reporters in the Gospel narratives." [1] Where are the Rationalists now? Their main purpose was to render Christian dogmas credible; and this has been done, so far as it has been done, not by explaining mysteries, but by deepening them. And Deism is quite as dead as its opponents. Voltaire is scarcely read except for amusement, and one has succeeded to his place and power whom Christianity, through the mouth of Schleiermacher, names a "rejected saint"—Spinoza.

If we are to name any single work of literature as having inaugurated that new view of religious questions

[1] Dr. Wace, in *The Nineteenth Century*, for May, 1889.

which makes the controversies of the last century look so futile to our eyes, it will assuredly be Lessing's " Education of the Human Race." He begins by inquiring whether a divine revelation must necessarily be a deliverance of absolute and final truth ? If not, is it therefore the less divine ? " Nothing," he says to the Deists, " in this best of [Leibnitzian] worlds deserves our contempt and dislike—and shall religion deserve it ? God has His hand in everything—only not in our errors ? " Let us consider revealed religion as an *education* in Truth,[1] and how natural and reasonable does its historical course at once appear ! It had been objected (by Reimarus, among others) that the Old Testament could not have been intended to convey a revelation, because it made no mention of the doctrine of immortality. But if the Jews were not then fit for the doctrine of immortality ? If the doctrine of immediate rewards and punishments was the only one which, in their then state of moral development, could have affected their conduct? The doctrine of immortality was first preached with authority by Christ, and He preached it only when the world was ready to receive it. So, too, the Jews were brought to believe in the Unity of God through being led to think of Him for many generations only as the most powerful among gods. And the very conception of the Unity of God has to expand into that of the multiplicity of God, which is indicated in the doctrine of the Trinity. A child is not taught scientific Truth at once—a wise teacher will use

[1] Johann Müller, the historian, observes that Lessing most pro- bably lit on this conception of religion as an educational process in his reading of the Fathers.

allegory, poetry, and other vehicles of Truth, knowing that in good time the pupil will learn to distinguish between the vehicle and the thing conveyed. Looked at in this light, what more perfect vehicle could be found for the conveyance of divine truths to a childish people than the Old Testament Scriptures?

With the fifty-fourth paragraph Lessing begins to apply this conception of revelation to the New Testament. Christ's mission seems to have been attested by wonders which won a vital belief for doctrines which would otherwise have remained mere philosophic speculations. But what are these wonders to us? We do not need them to confirm our faith. We have linked the revelations of Christ with truths of the Reason, and they are not now imperilled if the miracles of Christ be disputed, as any historical event may be. And the revelations themselves —are not the doctrines of Original Sin, of the Atonement, of the Trinity, as commonly understood, but vehicles for the conveyance of conceptions still more profound? The " Education of the Human Race " is not yet complete. Christian dogma itself—and here is the fundamental distinction between Lessing and the Rationalists—is but a stage from which higher levels may be attained.

He concludes by suggesting that each individual man must pass through the whole educational process the existence of which can only be perceived in the universal history of the race. Nay, this individual development may really be the cause of the general development—the great, slow-moving wheel of Time may be set in motion by a multitude of smaller wheels, each of which adds its quota to produce the visible result. Is one earthly life all that each of us can have? May not the same soul inhabit body after body, coming nearer and nearer to its divine aim with every transmigration? "Is this hypothesis to be ridiculed simply because it was the first which the human understanding embraced before it was weakened and distracted by the sophistries of the schools?"

The introduction into European thought of this view of religion as a *progressive revelation*, was probably the most important event in its own sphere which had taken place since the Reformation. It dissolved all the old parties, it emptied of meaning all the old issues, and for the old crude differences it substituted new ones, which gave room for the presence of a reconciling sympathy unknown and impossible before. And the form of Lessing's treatise, with its brief pregnant paragraphs and its occasional utterances of reverent and exalted piety, is worthy of what it had to convey.

The first fifty-three paragraphs of this work were published among the " Objections " to Reimarus, but the complete work did not appear till 1780. Enough, however, was indicated in the portion published in the "Objections" to make Lessing's general position clear in the long controversies in which he was henceforth immersed.

Before, however, we turn to deal with these we have to record the "insupportable and touching loss" which he suffered in the death of his wife. On Christmas Eve, 1777, she gave birth to a boy, who, although apparently healthy, died after twenty-four hours. Eva's confinement had been exceedingly severe :

"I seize," he wrote to Eschenburg, on the 31st, "a moment when my wife lies quite unconscious, to thank you for your kind interest. My joy was but short. And I lost him so unwillingly—this son! For he had so much sense—so much sense! . . . Was it not sense that they had to drag him into the world with iron tongs? that he marked the wretchedness of it so soon? Was it not sense that he seized the first opportunity to escape from it? And the little rascal tears his mother away with him. For there is still but little hope that she may be spared to me. I wanted at last to have as good a life of it as other men. But it has turned out badly for me."

Eva lay unconscious, or recognizing her husband alone, for nine or ten days; and he had often to be drawn from her bedside, lest the thought that she was leaving him should add to the pain of her last hour. At last there seemed a hope of her recovery, but it was only a transient one. On the 10th of January he wrote to Eschenburg a letter in which the anguish of a great sorrow speaks through the reserve of his stern self-control.

"My wife is dead, and I have now had this experience too. I am glad that few more such experiences can remain for me, and am quite calm."

A few days later he wrote to Karl in Berlin :—

"If you had known her! They say it is nothing but self-praise to praise one's wife. Well, I will say no more of her. But if you had known her! Never again, I fear, will you see me as our friend Moses did, so calm, so contented within my four walls."

But he was not the man to waste his heart in fruitless repining. Happily for him, a task had just been laid upon him which honour and duty forbade him to lay aside as long as life and intellect remained.

CHAPTER XIV

H ERMANN SAMUEL REIMARUS, Professor of
Oriental Languages at Hamburg, and author of
several philosophic books which had much popularity in
their day, had devoted twenty years of his life to a work,
the existence of which was kept profoundly secret, on
the Religion of Reason. In it the historic evidences of
Christianity were minutely discussed, and the origin of
that religion traced to deliberate fraud. His main attack
was directed against the main fortress of Christianity—the
doctrine of the Resurrection. Reimarus adduced in his
discussion of the subject ten "irreconcilable contradictions" in the Gospel narratives of that event, and argued
that narratives so inconsistent with each other were unworthy of credence. To account for the fact that the early
Christian belief in the Resurrection was not at once
exploded by the production of the body of Christ, he
suggests that the account current among the Jews, that
the disciples had stolen the body from the sepulchre,
represents what actually took place.

This work, entitled "An Apology for the Rational
Worshippers of God," had not been intended by its
author to see the light so soon. At first, indeed, it had

not been intended for publication at all—it was, he states, simply for the settlement of his own perplexities that he had begun to set down the reasonings which were leading him to doubt the received doctrines of Christianity. And his last desire with respect to the completed work, which he bequeathed to his son, a doctor of medicine in Hamburg, was that it should "remain in secret for the use of understanding friends . . . until the times had grown more enlightened." "Rather," he wrote, "let the masses remain in error for a while than that I, albeit innocently, should irritate them with truths which may set them in a fury of religious zeal." That the MS. was, in fact, allowed to explode in times which by no means fulfilled its author's idea of adequate enlightenment, appears to have been no fault of its inheritor; for when, so late as 1814, Dr. Reimarus presented a copy of the then famous MS. to the University of Göttingen, he requested that it might be reserved for the use of "fitting persons," and not lent for perusal to the general public. But Elise Reimarus, a woman of high cultivation and one of Lessing's truest and worthiest friends, had given him, while in Hamburg, a copy of a large portion of her father's "Apology," with permission to publish it as he should see fit, strict secresy being observed as to the author's name. And Dr. Reimarus made no objection, or as good as none, to this course.

Lessing was profoundly stirred by the perusal of this MS., and knew no rest till he had given it to the world. "I could not," he writes in his "Objections," "live in the same house with him." The criticism of Reimarus had raised doubts with which it was high time for Protestant

theology to grapple.   The early Reformers, in rejecting
the authority of the Church, had simply substituted that
of the Scriptures.   But it was impossible that Protestantism could rest there.   A Protestant Church which
should demand proofs from the Papacy, and at the same
time claim the right to substitute denunciation for discussion in dealing with its own recusants, must clearly
fail, in the long run, to hold the allegiance of all minds
whose allegiance was worth having.   And this was very
much what Lutheranism had done.   Controversy on the
truths of Christianity had meant that some wretched
Johann Schmidt or other would take his discovery of
some incredibility in the Pentateuch, some disagreement
in the Evangelists, to be worth ten times as much as it was,
just because he was forbidden to utter it—would fling it
at last with a shriek of defiance in the face of the orthodox world, would be answered by a counter-shriek in no
way more intelligent, and would presently find himself
meditating on the Rights of Man in the dungeon of some
Protestant prince.   Now Lessing had found in Reimarus
an open antagonist of Christianity whose polemic, far
from being delivered in a half-terrified, half-furious
scream, was composed with deliberation and temperance,
supported by solid learning, and expressed with an energy
and felicity of phrase which gave colour to the supposi-
tion (not yet quite extinct), that Lessing was himself the
author both of the " Fragments " and the " Objections."
Here, writes Lessing, we have almost an "ideal antagonist " of Christianity—can he fail to raise up a defender
worthy of him ?

Lessing's first attempt to publish the " Fragments "

was made in 1771, and they were duly submitted to the theological censorship in Berlin. But Berlin would tolerate only *sottises* against religion, and the censor refused his *Vidi*. Two years afterwards he published a Fragment, "On the Toleration of Deists," in the Wolfenbüttel Contributions, which was not likely to create, and did not create, any stir in the theological world. Further extracts were promised, and they came in the same vehicle in 1777, in the shape of five Fragments—(1) "On the Denunciation of Reason in the Pulpits"; (2) "The Impossibility of a Revelation which all men can believe on grounds of Reason"; (3) "The Passage of the Israelites through the Red Sea"; (4) "That the Books of the Old Testament were not written to reveal a Religion"; (5) "On the Accounts of the Resurrection." A final Fragment, "On the Aims of Jesus and His Disciples," was published separately in 1778.

The most important of those published in the "Contributions" were the second and the fifth. Reimarus, in the second, argues at great length, and with great acuteness, that however convincing a Revelation might be to those who first received it, it could never be a subject of rational religious belief to others who had to take it from tradition or documentary evidence. In the fifth Fragment the accounts of the Resurrection were sought to be discredited on the grounds of their discrepancies; and the last Fragment was written to show that Jesus and His disciples aimed first at the establishment of an earthly kingdom, and that the character of the Christian propaganda was only altered when His death put an end to these mundane hopes.

Lessing bears witness to the deep impression which the learning, penetration, and earnestness of his "Fragmentist" had made on him, and in his "Objections" indicates the defence which might be made against his arguments. In discussing the Fragment on the Impossibility of Revelation he admits the author's contention as against the common view of Revelation, but suggests a new view in the first part of the "Education of the Human Race."[1] In dealing with the Resurrection he admits the existence of the discrepancies alleged by the Fragmentist, but denies his conclusion from them. They refute, not the doctrine of the Resurrection, but only a certain theory of Inspiration. Why should we suppose the sacred writers to be infallible in all their utterances ? Is it conceivable that under the influence of inspiration they found themselves writing down things which they had not become aware of by the ordinary methods of observation and inquiry? Inspiration, he urges, is not mechanical but moral. The Evangelists were filled with a spirit which prompted them to write according to their best knowledge and conscience, but it did not guard them against the errors to which the sincerest witnesses are liable. And the discrepancies in the accounts of the Resurrection are just those, and no greater than those, which any collection of honest narratives of the same historical

[1] Lessing here communicates this work as ostensibly taken from the MS. of another writer, which has come into his hands. The same fiction was maintained when the whole treatise was published, and the theory started by Körte, in 1839, that t was really the work of one Thaer, and not Lessing's at all, had at one time many adherents. This view, however, has been exploded by Guhrauer, and needs no further discussion.

fact might be expected to exhibit. Then there is the great argument for Christianity that it is *there*. It proved its case in the opinion of contemporaries—shall we at this distance of time undertake to revise that judgment on the strength of trifling discrepancies in the evidence? In short, argues Lessing, the letter is not the spirit—the Bible is not religion. And objections to the letter and the Bible are not objections to religion. There was a Christianity before a single book of our New Testament existed. There might still be a Christianity if all the books of our New Testament were destroyed. It does not rest upon them—it is not true because the Apostles and Evangelists taught it, but they taught it because it was true. If any one thinks otherwise—if any one will contend for the literal infallibility of the Scriptures, let him answer the Fragmentist's objections to the Resurrection —but let him *answer* them, and answer them *all !*

Lessing, of course, neither expected nor desired that the "Fragments" should remain unattacked. The first assault was delivered by the Herr Director Schumann, of the Lyceum in Hanover, who, in 1777, published a treatise "On the Evidence of the Proofs of the Christian Religion." Here the fulfilment of the Messianic prophecies, and the miracles wrought by Jesus and His apostles, are offered as "proofs of the Spirit and the Power." Lessing, in his brief and courteous reply ("Ueber den Beweis des Geistes und der Kraft"), points out that fulfilled prophecies, accomplished miracles, are one thing—*reports* of them are quite different things. The reports may be believed, in the sense in which those of Alexander's Asiatic conquests are believed—but would any one make the history of Alexander the basis of a religion? Will any one regard any historical event as a truth so central, so unshakable, so profound, as to be the very criterion of all other knowledge? For nothing less than this a religious truth must be.

The Archdeacon and Superintendent Ress, of Wolfen-büttel, was Lessing's next opponent. His "Defence of the Account of the Resurrection" appeared anonymously in Brunswick shortly after Schumann's treatise, and attempted a refutation in detail of all the contradictions adduced by the Fragmentist, whom Ress treated as a shallow sophist. Lessing replied in "A Rejoinder" ("Eine Duplik"), in which he denounced Ress's method of defending the infallibility of the Evangelists by treating their statements as so many "noses of wax," which could be squeezed into any meaning that a gratuitous theological assumption might render desirable. He went through Ress's explanations one by one, and showed in every case, with one exception, that on any natural system of interpretation they were entirely inadequate. The "Duplik" also contained a scornful warning to persons of the calibre of Ress to beware how they treated with arrogance and contempt an opponent such as the Fragmentist, the worthy and learned thinker of whose identity Lessing now abandons all pretence of ignorance.[1]

The cloud of foes whom the "Fragments" brought

[1] The name was, however, still kept carefully concealed. Lessing was at one time strongly desirous of publishing it, as the best answer to those who thought they could treat the Fragmentist with contempt; but the Reimarus family would not hear of it.

into the field soon thickened. Rationalists like Semler made common cause with the orthodox against them; and Lessing's brother has reckoned, apart from innumerable pamphlets and newspaper articles, no less than thirty-two separate works, some of them of considerable size, which were launched against Lessing and the "Fragments" in the years 1778 and 1779 alone. Plainly Protestant Germany was in earnest about its religion. Unhappily, however, the tone of the controversy soon degenerated. Goeze, the Chief Pastor of Hamburg, whom we have seen on friendly terms with Lessing in that city, published—first in a newspaper, afterwards in a volume ("Herr Hofrath Lessing's Direct and Indirect Attacks on the Christian Religion and the Scriptures")—a number of essays on the "Fragments" and their editor, in which Lessing was accused of treacherously endeavouring, by a show of reasonableness and impartiality, to capture public favour for the blasphemous absurdities of the Fragmentist; and followed up this attack with a criticism entitled "Lessing's Weaknesses." This was certainly not the ideal defender of Christianity whom Lessing had hoped that Reimarus would call forth; but he was typical of a large class, and Lessing chose him out for combat as the most redoubtable champion of his side. His intolerant vituperative tone, his insolence towards Reimarus (whose sincerity and learning Lessing was bound in honour to defend to the utmost of his power), and particularly his hint to the civil authorities that the cause of social order was involved in the contest, stirred Lessing to the very depths; and never did a Chief Pastor receive such an Olympian

castigation as that which followed.   Week after week
Lessing dealt with him and other antagonists in a little
brochure entitled "Anti-Goeze" — eleven in all—and
so marvellous was his use of all the resources of
controversy that Goeze was at last fairly argued, or awed,
into silence.   Lessing's strokes were delivered with the
arm of a giant, and guided by the eye of a lynx.   His
vast and exact learning, his trained dramatic faculty, his
mastery of style, the breadth and inner harmony of the
critical and religious theories which he unfolded, in his
usual manner, out of a petty difference about the contradictions in the Evangelists, made the solitary thinker
more than a match for all the schools of Protestant
Germany.   Like Frederick in the Seven Years' War, he
seemed to multiply himself to meet the multitude of his
enemies.   And, like Frederick, he was no mere warrior.
If he sometimes fought for a territory of barren soil he
soon transformed it to a flourishing colony of Thought,
and made his conquest irrecoverably sure.   His courage
and resource were unbounded.   It was in the thick
of the struggle that he issued the last Fragment of
Reimarus—"On the Aims of Jesus and His Disciples "
—the surest of all, as he well knew, to excite his powerful
and dangerous antagonists to the last extreme of indignation.   Finally, when a decree of arbitrary power silenced
his voice among the throng of disputants, it was soon
heard to descend from unassailable heights of art, pro-
claiming thence in rarer and sweeter tones the forbidden
gospel of charity and reason.

CHAPTER XV

ALL the "Anti-Goezes" had issued without objection from the ducal printing-house. Lessing, by special favour, had possessed the privilege of having his works published there without having to submit them to the ordeal of inspection by the censorship. But he seems never to have anticipated that this privilege could be revoked; and was amazed and indignant to find that, in the absence of his special protector, the Hereditary Prince, the old Duke was worked upon, by the outcries of Lessing's lay and clerical enemies (who acted through the Lutheran Consistorium of Brunswick), to forbid the director of the ducal printing-office to print anything further of Lessing's which had not been approved by the censorship, or to continue to publish the last two "Fragments." "What a triumph for Goeze," he wrote, and in a few days he turned to the Duke with a respectful application to be allowed to continue his polemic, seeing, as he said, that he had been attacked by Goeze with a fury compared with which the worst that he had ever uttered was simply complimentary! It was true that he had engaged, when granted the freedom of publication, to print nothing which could be an offence to religion or morals; but he had understood this as meaning that he was to utter nothing in his own person, and as his own

opinion, which could so offend—not that he should be
guided by religious considerations in selecting which
of the treasures of the Library should be made public;
and he challenged the most scrupulous theologian to
point out a sentence in his own writings which could lay
him open to the charge of holding unorthodox views.
This petition was presented on the 11th of July, 1778.
On the 13th the Duke signed a mandate requiring
Lessing to send in within eight days the MS. of the
"Fragments," to surrender his title to freedom of the
censorship, and to refrain from all further publication of
the " Fragments," or of similar writings.

How Lessing's proud and restless spirit must have
chafed at finding his hands thus fettered in the midst
of so momentous a combat, may easily be imagined, and
how he must have longed for " the glorious privilege of
being independent," which would have permitted him to
fling the yoke of Wolfenbüttel to the winds.   Indeed,
he wrote about this time to Eschenburg, saying that,
although the confiscation of the " Fragments " was a
matter of little moment to him, he positively must and
would resign his position if the prohibition against continuing the polemic with Goeze were insisted on.

On the 3rd of August arrived the answer to Lessing's
petition.   It strictly forbade all reproduction of the
" Anti-Goezes," and all publication of future writings
without the consent of the Ministry.   Lessing was now
nearly beaten to the pit.   It seemed as if no choice
lay before him but a dishonourable surrender, or the
resignation of a post which he could ill afford to lose.
But there was still a course by which both parties

might have their legitimate claims satisfied. The prohibition as regards future publications, he wrote on
August 8th, was surely only intended to apply to
publications within the territory of the Duke of Brunswick. Otherwise he had already contravened it ; his
" Necessary Answer to a Very Unnecessary Question of
Herr Pastor Goeze " (viz., what Lessing meant by the
Christian religion, and what religion he professed himself?), had already gone to Berlin to be printed, having
duly passed the censorship there. The Duke's advisers
would have none of this compromise. *Nowhere* was
Lessing to continue his controversy without consent of
the Ministry of Brunswick. Now the issue was clear at
last—now it seemed as if Lessing's enemies must either
deal him the one crushing blow which they had it in their
power to administer, or he disarm them by unconditional
surrender. But the cloud proved to have no lightning in
it ; the Consistorium turned out to be chiefly an affair of
painted pasteboard when confronted by a man resolved
not to take words for realities. Lessing published his
" Necessary Answer," pointing to the creeds of the
Church as the authoritative exposition of Christian
doctrine. And on what did the creeds themselves rest?
Not on the Scriptures, argued Lessing, but on that oral
tradition which preceded all the New Testament Scriptures, and which was regarded by the early Christians as
a higher source of truth than any written document.
And the " Necessary Answer " was soon succeeded by
an " Erste Folge " (printed in Hamburg), which ex-
posed Goeze's misconstruction of a crucial passage in
Irenæus, advanced to combat Lessing's view of the

position of the New Testament in the early Church,
and which arrayed citation after citation from the
Fathers in support of the thesis of the previous work.
The Consistorium did not, or could not move, and
this "first sequel" never had a second, for Goeze
was silenced at last, and Lessing could now obey the
Duke's mandate without humiliation, if not without
reluctance.   So closed this momentous controversy—
the most momentous, on the whole, which had agitated
Europe since Luther published his Theses.   It had
vindicated the claims of the individual intellect, as
Luther had vindicated those of the individual conscience; and the vindication had been accomplished by
no reckless and narrow enthusiast, but by a sober, far-
seeing, and scholarly thinker.   Towards his opponents
Lessing is often vehement and scornful, but his tone in
speaking of the religion of which they constituted themselves the defenders is always deeply reverent.   In fact,
he was endeavouring to clear a way by which men of
intellect and candour could approach it.   The beautiful
motto from the " Ion " of Euripides, which, with the
change of " Phœbus " to " Christ," he prefixed to an
unfinished writing on " Bibliolatry," describes the part
which he sincerely thought himself to be playing in this
controversy, and the spirit in which he played it :—

> " How lovely is the service, Christ,
> Wherewith before Thy temple doors
> I honour the prophetic seat." [1]

In this controversy Lessing dealt both with Christianity
as a religious system, and with the documents which

[1] Spoken by Ion, as he sweeps the threshold of Apollo's temple.

attest its origin; and in each sphere he produced an epoch-making work. The first of these was the " Education of the Human Race." The other was a tract on "A New Hypothesis Concerning the Evangelists, regarded as merely Human Writers," first published in a collection of his posthumous theological writings, in 1784. "I do not think," he wrote to Karl, in February, 1778, "that I have ever written anything more sound and complete in this line; or, I may add, more ingenious." He starts with drawing attention to the existence of the body of Jewish Christians indicated in Acts xxiv. 5, who were called "Nazarenes," and who formed the very earliest Christian Church. In this first of the Churches, it was natural to suppose, the first written account of the life and teaching of Christ would be produced. And this account would form the basis for all subsequent writings on the same subject. Now, is there any evidence of the existence of such a Jewish Gospel?

There is evidence the most abundant and indisputable. Between the first and the fifth centuries we have a group of Fathers, ending with Jerome, who make mention of a "Hebrew," (*i.e.*, Syro-Chaldaic) Gospel. It is spoken of as the Gospel of the Hebrews, or sometimes as the Gospel according to Matthew, described as the only Gospel received by the Jewish Christians, and quoted always as a high authority, and sometimes as an inspired work. St. Jerome, who translated it into Latin and Greek, observes that it was often used by Origen, and quotes it himself with approval.[1] Here, then, Lessing argues, we have the origin of the canonical Gospels. Matthew's Gospel was

[1] Mr. E. B. Nicholson has put together all that is known about

the first Greek translation of such parts of the Nazarene Gospel as Matthew saw fit to use; hence the fact that the less known original sometimes passed under his name. Mark and Luke represent other partial versions of the same original. But this original took its form among men who had known our Lord personally during His earthly life, and who reported little of Him which might not have been told of a mere man, albeit one en-dowed with marvellous powers from on high. The Fourth Gospel was then written by John to represent Christ from the side of His Godhead. There are in reality only two Gospels—that represented by the Synoptics, which is the Gospel of the Flesh; and that of John, which is the Gospel of the Spirit. And to the latter it is due that Christianity became a world-wide religion instead of perishing as a Jewish sect.

Critics of authority differ as to the positive value of Lessing's "New Hypothesis," but all are agreed in reckoning its appearance as the birth of a new science. It discredited, not by argument, but by showing what could be achieved in disregard of them, the old theories of mechanical inspiration. It inaugurated the great investigations of nineteenth century theology into the origins of the canon, and the currents of thought which prevailed in the early Christian Churches.

It is quite certain, for Lessing has himself admitted it, that in these religious controversies he often "chose his weapons according to his opponents"—that his

this Gospel in his treatise on "The Gospel according to the Hebrews," (Kegan, Paul, & Co., 1879). About thirty fragments of it remain, showing very marked affinity to the Gospel of St. Matthew.

defence, on certain hypotheses, of a certain view did not always represent his own opinion of it. Goeze, as we have seen, demanded that Lessing should declare unambiguously his own personal view of the Christian religion ; and Lessing, in a letter to Elise Reimarus, congratulates himself on being able to avoid doing this by taking Goeze as asking merely *what he understood* by that religion. And this question Lessing answers by pointing to the three creeds as the authoritative expression of Christian doctrine. Goeze was apparently satisfied, but posterity has not allowed Lessing to escape in this way, and the question of his religious opinions has been closely investigated by many critics. Yet it cannot be said to have been completely set at rest. The fact seems to be that Lessing, in his later years, had reached a stage of philosophical development in which the expression of final truth on these subjects is seen to be impossible. And hence all positive religions, which exist by their endeavour to express the inexpressible, were to him at once true and false. His attitude towards Christianity had certainly changed very markedly since he wrote his treatise on the "Bacchanalia." His final view of it is probably represented, as far as it is capable of representation, in a Fragment published among his posthumous works, the date of which is unknown, but which appears to be an attempt to answer, purely for his own satisfaction, the question addressed to him by Goeze.

"I have," he writes, "nothing against the Christian religion ; on the contrary, I am its friend, and shall remain well-disposed and attached to it all my life. It answers the purpose of a positive religion as well as any other. I believe it, and hold it to be true, as much as one can believe and hold to be true any historical fact whatever." . . . With this declaration (says Lessing) the Rationalists ought to be contented; and as for those who hold Christian belief to be a thing *sui generis* produced by the direct influence of the Holy Spirit, " I cannot deny the possibility of this direct influence of the Holy Spirit, and assuredly would wilfully do nothing which could hinder this possibility from becoming a reality.

" Certainly I must confess. . . ."

And so ends the Fragment. Lessing never went nearer to expressing his final conclusions on this subject.

The struggle with the Consistorium once over, Lessing left Wolfenbüttel with his step-daughter, " Malchen," for a visit to Hamburg (September 12, 1778). He had meant only to stay a week, but did in fact remain more than a month. After the period of suffering and strife he had lately passed through, his spirit now found a much needed refreshment in the society of friends who could give him not only their affection but their intellectual sympathy. Chief among these was now Elise Reimarus; but we find also the names of Bode, Claudius, and the great translator, Voss, among those with whom pleasant hours were passed. But they marked with pain that Lessing's robust frame was beginning to show signs of feebleness. Some of his old vivacity and vigour was wanting—he had frequent slight indispositions—in particular it was noticed that, even in the midst of company, he was liable to strange fits of drowsiness. Towards the end of October he returned to Wolfenbüttel, and there devoted himself to giving its final form to the great dramatic poem with which he hoped to deal the forces of intolerance and unreason a heavier blow than he could " with ten more Fragments."

CHAPTER XVI

O N the 11th of August, 1778, Lessing wrote to his brother Karl :—

"Many years ago I sketched out a drama whose subject has a kind of analogy with these present controversies, which I little dreamt of then. If you and Moses think well of it, I shall have the thing printed by subscription, and you can print and distribute the enclosed announcement as soon as possible."

The announcement informs the public that, as Lessing has been compelled to " desist from a work which he has not carried on with that pious cunning with which alone it can be carried on successfully," he has been led by chance to take up an old dramatic attempt, and give it the last finishing touches. He begs his friends throughout Germany to procure subscribers for the work, and to let him know by Christmas the result of their efforts. The price was fixed at about one gulden.

To Elise he wrote that he was writing his play in verse, " for the sake of speed "; and the metre chosen was the English ten-syllabled blank verse—a form never before used in German for a work of such importance, but which thenceforth became the accepted dramatic metre of that language, as it is in English.

It was natural that the announcement of a new drama by the author who had given the German

stage its first great comedy, and its first great
tragedy, should excite much interest. And of course
this interest was heightened by the suspicion that
" Nathan the Wise " would be in some sense a continuation of that religious polemic by which Germany had
been so deeply stirred. Accordingly the efforts of
Lessing's friends (and no man ever had more faithful and
helpful friends) rapidly swelled the list of subscribers.
Elise alone obtained over seventy names in a couple of
months. Herder, who had learned to know and admire
Lessing in Hamburg, announced twenty-six. Even
persons entirely unknown to Lessing collected names,
and by January, 1779, more than a thousand were
announced, which had risen to 1,200 in the following
April, besides many orders from the booksellers. The
plan of publishing by subscription, which others besides
Lessing were then adopting, had the great advantage of
circumventing the book pirates, from whom authors were
then suffering so much ; and Lessing, who, as usual, was
deep in debt, had need of all the profit his brains could
bring him.

In April, after months of quiet and careful work, all
was ready for the press—as ready, at least, as Lessing's
works ever were when first put in type—and "Nathan"
appeared about the middle of May.

The reader will hardly expect to find a great work of
art in a drama avowedly produced as an episode in a
theological controversy. Nor probably has "Nathan"
had many readers who will agree with Düntzer's assertion
that, were it not for Lessing's own declarations, no one
would suspect the piece to be written with any polemical

purpose. The propagandist character of the drama, ethical or speculative, is stamped on every page of it. How could it be otherwise with a work of which its author wrote, that he would be content "if it taught one reader in a thousand to doubt the evidence and universality of his religion?"[1] Lessing, indeed, does himself injustice in this utterance, for although his drama is certainly and recognizably a "Tendenzstück," it is written in no spirit of doubt, nor is it such a spirit that it could tend to nourish in its readers. Rather is it calculated to appease the pain of doubts which may have already arisen, by pointing to unsuspected possibilities of a wider and nobler belief. The insolence and intolerance of the orthodoxy of Lessing's day are indeed portrayed with a polemical emphasis in the character of the Patriarch; but the drama contains worthier representatives of Christianity than this ecclesiastic, and the famous parable of the Three Rings goes rather to show how well a man may serve God in any religion, than how little he can place his faith in one.

But, unquestionably, one of the means by which Lessing in this play tries to combat intolerance and folly, is the weaning of men's minds from the contemplation of earthly things in the light of theological assumptions. The evil attending this attitude of mind is exhibited in different forms, as it makes itself manifest in different types of character. We perceive it in Recha as a useless and aimless enthusiasm; in the Templar, as a cold spiritual pride; in the Patriarch, as a furious bigotry which has killed every sentiment of charity and rectitude.

[1] To Karl Lessing, April 18, 1779.

Recha, the enthusiast, a Christian by birth and baptism, is the adopted daughter of the wealthy Jew Nathan, to whose protection she was brought as an infant on the day on which he hears the news that his own wife and family have been slaughtered in an outbreak of Christian bigotry. She and her supposed father are represented as living in Jerusalem in the time of the great Sultan Saladin. The latter has recently taken prisoner a number of Templars, all of whom are condemned to die, save one who is saved by his singular resemblance to a loved and long-lost brother of Saladin's. The Christian youth and maiden are brought together by an accident. The house of Nathan takes fire in the absence of its owner on a trading expedition to the East—Recha is in imminent danger of a fearful death, when the young Templar, who has been attracted to the spot by the crowd, flings his white mantle before his face, rushes into the flames, and bears her out in safety. Nathan returns with his caravan of costly wares, learns the danger which the creature he most loves on earth has so narrowly escaped, and longs to thank her saviour. But he finds the young Templar holding aloof, in a spirit of inhuman contempt, from the Jewish family he has so deeply served, while Recha, and her Christian companion Daja, will not have her deliverer to be a man at all—he was an angel, and the white mantle is transformed by her ecstatic fancy into his protecting wings. Thus at the very outset of the play its philosophic drift is indicated. It is Nathan's part to *humanize* the ideas both of the Templar and of Recha ; and the reader will note how admirably here, as elsewhere, Lessing has fused the intellectual with the æsthetic interest of his drama. Everywhere Thought leads to Action, and because we are made aware of this, the former wins that vital interest for us which nothing else could give it; although it must be confessed that, as is usual in works of this kind, what Thought gains Action loses.

Here, in a somewhat abridged form, is the powerful scene in which Nathan corrects the devout raptures of Recha :—

> *Recha.* . . . Visibly he came,
> Visibly bore me through the flames. I felt
> The wind of his white wings—yea, I too, father,
> Have seen an angel, seen him face to face.
> *My* angel.
> *Nathan.* Was not Recha worth his help ?
> Nor saw she aught more beautiful in him
> Than he, perchance, in her.
> *Recha* (smiling).   You flatter, father,
> Me? or the angel?
> *Nathan.*   Yet were it a man,
> A common man, e'en such as every day
> Kind Nature sends, that did this deed for thee,
> Still were that common man in truth God's angel.
> *Recha.* What? Nay, not such an angel, not indeed
> A very angel. Father, have not you,
> Even you yourself, taught me full many a time
> That angels are ? that God for those who love Him
> Works wonders? And I love Him.
> *Nathan.*   And He thee.
> And He for thee, and beings such as thou,
> Works wonders every hour. . . .
> My Recha, was't not miracle enough
> That a mere man should save thee, one indeed
> Whom no small miracle had saved for this ?

When was it told till now that Saladin
Had spared a Templar? that a Templar ever
Had begged, had hoped for mercy? offered ransom
More than the leathern belt that trails his sword,
Or, at the most, his poniard? . . .

        Hear me now!

This being, be it angel, be it man,
That saved thee, him would ye, and thou in special
My Recha, serve, how gladly and how well!
Is it not so? Now, for an angel, mark,
What can ye do? what recompense afford?
Thank him, and sigh to him, and pray to him,
Pour out your hearts in ecstasy for him,
Fast on his day, give alms—'Tis nothing all!
Ye, and your neighbours are the better of it,
Not *he*. Your fasting will not feed him, nor
Your alms enrich him, nor your raptures raise,
Nor is he aught the mightier for your faith.
Is it not so? But—if it were a man——!

 Daja. Truly we had more chance to serve him then!
God knows how gladly we had done it too!
But he would naught of us—himself alone
Sufficed himself, as only angels can.

 Recha. And when at last he vanished . . .

 Nathan.   Vanished? he?
Saw you him not again beneath the palms?
Nor sought him once again?

 Daja.   Sought him? not we.

 Nathan. Not sought him? Daja! not? What have ye done?
Ah! cruel in your raptures that ye are!
—How if this angel now were sick?

 Recha.   Were sick?

 Daja. Sick? God forbid.

 Recha.   Daja! how chill I grow!
I tremble. Feel my forehead, once so warm.
'Tis ice.

 Nathan. He is a Frank; the climate strange;
Young; unaccustomed to the toils of war.

Recha. Sick—sick—

Daja. He only means, 'tis possible.

Nathan. Now lies he there, and hath nor friends, nor gold
Wherewith to purchase friends——

Recha. Ah, father! father!

Nathan. Lies all untended, counsel none, nor cheer;
The prey of pain and death, now lies he there——

Recha. Where? where?

Nathan. And he for one he never knew,
One that he never saw—enough for *him*
To know that 'twas a human creature—hurled
Himself into the flames.

Daja. Ah, Nathan, spare her!

Nathan. He that would even spare the thing he saved
The burden of thanksgiving——

Daja. Have pity, Nathan!

Nathan. Nor ever sought to see her face again,
—Unless perchance she were to save again—
Enough for him, that 'twas a fellow man!

Daja. Nathan, for pity's sake be silent; see her!

Nathan. He, *he* lies dying in his lonely pain,
Refreshed but by remembrance of this deed.

Daja. Cease! will you slay her?

Nathan. And hast thou not slain,
Or could'st have slain, thy saviour? Recha, Recha,
'Tis medicine and not poison that I give thee.
He lives—come to thyself! he lives indeed.
For aught I know he is not even sick.
Not even sick.

Recha. For sure? not dead? not sick?
Not dead for sure?

Nathan. Good deeds done here below
Even here doth God requite. Go! thou hast marked
How easy is religious ecstasy,
How hard right action! How the veriest sluggard
Will love to wander in such ecstasies
Only—and oftentimes I think he knows
His motives but obscurely—not to hear
His conscience bid him act!

Was ever the dramatic form more finely used for the expression of moral ideas ? With what power, for instance, even the agonized *silence* of Recha, as she realizes the selfishness of her enthusiasm, is conveyed to us !

The Templar is next sought out by Nathan, who softens his crude obstinacy with equal skill. Only the Patriarch, the representative of bigotry in its harshest form, who wishes to have Nathan burnt for bringing up Recha in ignorance of her religion, is left untouched by the influence of the wise Jew. He has no part in the action of the piece, and, though he supplies a needed ethical contrast, is dramatically useless.

The central scene of the play exhibits the solvent and sweetening power of Nathan's philosophy in the sphere of speculation, just as in the scenes with Recha and the Templar we have the same power exercised in the sphere of conduct. Saladin has asked Nathan, as a man of deep and inquiring mind, to tell him candidly which of the three religions represented in Jerusalem he holds to be the true one. As answer Lessing places in Nathan's mouth an ingenious and beautiful adaptation of the Boccaccian fable of the Three Rings. A man of the East, who lived " many grey years ago," had a wondrous opal ring, in which lay the mysterious power of making acceptable in God's sight any possessor who wore it in this faith. It descended in one family from son to son, according to the rule of the original possessor that it should always go to the best-beloved, until at last one father who had three equally beloved sons, and had promised it to each in turn, caused two new rings to be made in exact imitation of the old, and secretly gave each son a ring which each understood to be the genuine and only one. He died, and each son at once produced his ring and claimed to be master of the house. They examined, they quarrelled, they argued—all in vain ; the true ring was undiscoverable. "Almost as undiscoverable," adds Nathan, "as the true faith."

Saladin is thunderstruck at this answer, and now Nathan proceeds to build up in another form what he had so ruthlessly thrown down. A wise judge is called in to decide the brothers' contention, and the essence of the judgment is to substitute humanism for super-naturalism. Which is the true ring he cannot tell—perhaps it may have been lost, and the father, to conceal the loss, may have had *three* copies made—perhaps he would no longer endure "the tyranny of the one ring" in his house :—

> " He loved you all and loved you all alike—
> Would not have one exalted, one oppressed—
> Mark that ! and be it yours to emulate
> His free impartial love ! Strive, each of you,
> To show the ring's benignant might his own ;
> Yea, help the mystic power to do its kind
> With gentleness, with loving courtesy,
> Beneficence, submissiveness to God.
> And when, full many a generation hence,
> Within your children's children's children's hearts
> The power of the ring is manifest,
> Lo! in a thousand thousand years again
> Before this judgment seat I summon you,
> Where one more wise than I shall sit and speak.
> Now go your way." So spake the modest judge.
> *Saladin.* God ! God !

Nathan.   And now, O Saladin, if thou
Art confident that thou indeed art he,
The wise, the promised judge . . .
   Saladin.   I, dust ? I, nothing ?'
O God !
   Nathan. What moves the Sultan ?
   Saladin.   Nathan, Nathan,
The thousand thousand years are not yet done.
Not mine that judgment seat ! Enough—farewell !
But henceforth be my friend."

Nothing can exceed the power with which, in this and
other passages in the play, the communication of thought
is painted from mind to kindling mind. And thought is
the main affair of the piece. It is full of wise and
weighty *sententiæ*, and the style has nothing of the
laconic energy of Lessing's prose dramas ; without being
exactly diffuse, it has an Oriental tranquillity and leisure
well suited to the subject and the scene. But as a
drama of action—and that is equivalent to saying, as a
drama—the piece has many and obvious faults. Except
for the wise, humane, calm and yet impassioned nature
of the Jew, and the quaint originality and independence
of his friend the Dervish, its personages have really
neither convictions nor character. The young Templar
who comes to Palestine to fight for the Holy Sepulchre
while disbelieving, apparently, in the Divinity of Christ ;
who is prejudiced enough to hold aloof from the family
of the Jew whose daughter he has rescued, and philosophic enough to be attracted by him when he finds him
to be merely a Deist who goes to the synagogue because
his fathers did ; who is enraged at the idea that this
enlightened and admirable Jew has brought up a Christian

infant in his own ideas ; and who flings his own Order and cause to the winds and enters Mussulman service, simply because Saladin has spared his life—there is certainly no more impossible figure in dramatic literature. One feels that he only holds together at all by virtue of the fiery temper which he carries with him into all his contradictions. And so dominant is the ethical and philosophical interest in the play, that Lessing has observed none of those rules in the construction of the plot which he insisted upon so forcibly in the *Hamburgische Dramaturgie.* Once the Templar has been won to visit Nathan, there is absolutely no point in the play to which the action tends, no dramatic *nodus* to be unloosed ; for the revelation of the Templar's kinship to Saladin and Recha has a purely ethical, not a dramatic significance. The progress of the Templar's love affair with Recha does indeed excite a certain interest the *first* time we witness it. But the plot of a good play should please us as much when we know the end as when we do not ; and who can watch with satisfaction the episodes in a love-tale in which he knows that the lovers will turn out to be brother and sister ? Lessing was more concerned to show us that it was his own kin from whom the Templar's religious prejudices were severing him, than to provide his drama with an artistically satisfying *dénouement.*

Lessing himself should have taught us better than to call " Nathan " a good drama ; but a bad drama may be a noble poem, and as such we shall not easily cease to love it.

CHAPTER XVII

I N spite of "Nathan," Lessing was not done with the theologians yet. Dr. Walch, the most eminent contemporary authority on Church history, came out about this time with a critical investigation into the use of the "New Testament among the Early Christians," and endeavoured to show, as against Lessing, that the Scriptures were the true "rule of faith" of the early Church. Lessing began his "Bibliolatrie" in reply, but, finding himself falling into a cumbrous and pedantic mode of treatment, he gave it up, and began instead a series of "Letters to Various Theologians," also another polemical drama, "The Pious Samaritan." Much was now begun, but nothing finished. Lessing's energy was visibly declining, his lethargic illness steadily increased, his eyes became affected, and there were days when he could not even read. He was again in money difficulties, too, for the proceeds of "Nathan" had largely gone to repay a loan to a Jewish friend named Wessely. The Protestant Estates of the Empire were now threatening to prosecute him before the Aulic Council for the publication of the "Fragments," and even the populace in Wolfenbüttel began to show their bigoted antipathy to the great and genial spirit who had made their little town a second Wittenberg. Lessing was pained and often depressed, but not soured—his friends never found him more helpful and kindly.

When they visited him at Wolfenbüttel they found, at this time (1779), installed there a strange pair, about whom there hangs a strange tale, not the least worthy to be recorded of the minor episodes of Lessing's life. One day there presented himself at Lessing's door an unkempt and shabbily-dressed individual, whom every one soon learned, from the example of Lessing's household, to speak of as "the philosopher." He was accompanied by a huge and equally wild and uncomely looking dog. The man's name was Köneman. "Who are you?" asked Lessing; and the ragged Köneman's simple reply, "I am a philosopher," was enough to open to him the door and the heart of such a lover of character and humour as Lessing. He had travelled from his native place, which turned out to be Lithuania, to seek employment as tutor in some wealthy family. But no wealthy family had seen fit to engage him, and now he had neither "Dach" nor "Fach"—home, nor work, nor bread. But he had something better—he had a purpose; and the visible attestation of it was a dirty MS. which he drew from under his coat. This was an unfinished philosophical work "On the Higher Destinies of the Human Race," (destinies to be reached partly by the destruction of all that had been so far evolved), which, it was to be expected, would create an epoch in history. Let Lessing give him a garret to sleep in, and enough food to keep body and soul together, while he finished his manuscript—this was the request he came to prefer. He got what he asked and more, being treated as Lessing always treated distress. But his sense of the transcendent merit of the revelation contained in the dirty MS. was too blind to permit him to profit by the best thing Lessing had to give—his criticism. When the latter ventured to point out certain grammatical blunders in the language of his work (which was not without some germs of thought), the philosopher answered that he meant to write a preface, in which it should be explained that he had not concerned himself about correctness in these trifling matters. Neither had he concerned himself to master the graces of good breeding; and he and his dog, (especially the dog), were very unpopular with Lessing's friends. But Lessing would neither part them nor part with them. The wild human had found and succoured the wild canine friend when both were almost *in extremis.* The man had two rolls of bread—his last; and he gave one to the other famishing outcast. "He shared honourably with the dog," said Lessing; "and as long as I have a crust, the philosopher shall have half of it." Köneman stayed several weeks with Lessing, working at his manuscript, and then proceeded to Erfurt, where his subsequent foolish proceedings do not concern us.

The old Duke Charles of Brunswick died in March, 1780, and Lessing's patron reigned in his stead. One of his first acts was to arrest an acquaintance of Lessing's, a Jew named Daveson, on a charge of presenting fraudulent accounts of debts due to him by the late Duke.

Even before his friendship with Mendelssohn, Lessing had championed the oppressed race, nor indeed was it only in Mendelssohn that he had found in it types of character and culture which impressed him profoundly. Wessely is supposed to have even furnished some traits for Nathan. Of Daveson's innocence Lessing was ardently and, as it turned out, quite justly convinced; and although it is admitted that the bearing of the Jew in the presence of the Duke had given the latter some just cause for offence, Lessing openly espoused his cause, visited him in prison, and even took him into his house when at last he was released in dejection and ill-health. The poor and oppressed never failed to find a helper in the man of whom it is reported that he could not walk the streets without being liable to insult from ignorant bigots, hounded on by learned ones. Gleim even wrote to Ebert after Lessing's death asking in great anxiety about reports which had reached him from Brunswick : it had been rumoured that Lessing had been murdered by some fanatic whom the outrageous calumnies of his opponents had armed against his life. Among the populace the fearful " Faust " legend was revived about the manner of Lessing's death. It was whispered that he had been carried straight to hell by the devil in person. These reports serve to show the kind of atmosphere in which Lessing's last days were spent. He had to write a tract defending himself against the charge of having been bribed with 1,000 ducats by the Jews of Amsterdam to publish the "Fragments." Elise tells him that he is in some quarters suspected of an illicit affection for his step-daughter, his much-loved Malchen, who kept

house for him; and that this is supposed to be the reason
why she is not yet married.

To so humane and affectionate a nature as Lessing's
the malignant enmity with which he was now surrounded
must have been painful, the more so because it rarely
manifested itself in any form with which he could fairly
grapple; and his sorrow and indignation told visibly on
his physical energies.   But his failing hands still held up
the standard of culture and freedom, and still the young
energies of Germany drew courage and guidance from
his spirit.   In Brunswick, where he had now hired rooms
in the Ægidean Platz, to occupy during his visits there,
his chief intimates were Eschenburg, who had a post in
the Carolinum, and Leisewitz.   The latter was a young
dramatic poet, who had formed himself on Lessing, and
whose drama, "Julius von Tarent," had earned his
master's warm approval.   Lessing even took it for a
work of the author of "Götz von Berlichingen."
Leisewitz, indeed, besides his striking and varied
capacity as an author, had a fine nature, one in which
gaiety and earnestness were very happily combined;
and his affection for Lessing was very deep.

Another admirer of Lessing's, who now comes upon the
scene for the first time, was Friedrich Jacobi.   Readers of
that most fascinating book, Goethe's "Dichtung und
Wahrheit," will remember the friend with whom Goethe
sat up all night at Düsseldorf, while they looked over the
moonlit Rhine and poured out to each other the passionate spiritual yearnings then stirring in so many young
hearts.   Goethe had found Jacobi riper than himself—
he was indeed several years older—and had found, too,

that nothing but his study of Spinoza enabled him in some measure to comprehend the thoughts of his new friend. Lessing, too, had been strongly attracted by Spinoza, and the conversations which took place between himself and Jacobi, during a visit of the latter to Wolfenbüttel in 1780, were destined to further very materially the great work to which so many forces were then contributing—the restoration to his true place and power of that long-neglected thinker. Jacobi published his records of these conversations shortly after Lessing's death, in order to prove that the latter was a thorough disciple of Spinoza. This position was warmly contested by Mendelssohn, and the question whether Leibnitz or Spinoza is to have the credit of Lessing's final allegiance is still a debated point.

Spinoza had taken up the philosophic problem where Descartes laid it down. Descartes assumed the existence of two distinct and independent substances, Mind and Matter, and had endeavoured in vain to find some principle of union, some vital relation between them. Spinoza did not indeed abolish the antithesis, but he made it subordinate to a deeper unity. Defining substance, or existence, as that which exists by and for itself alone, he deduced the conclusion that there can be but one substance; for absolute, spontaneous, self-creating existence implies infinity, and there can be but one infinite. This one infinite substance Spinoza named God. Thought and Matter are but attributes of it. The question, then, how Thought and Matter can act on each other has disappeared—if we are thinking in the category of matter, all is matter, if in that of spirit, all is spirit. The correspondence which exists between them is like that which exists between the area of a circle and the mathematical line which limits it. For practical purposes they are different things, yet they are in reality but one and the same thing—the circle, regarded in different aspects.

Mind and Matter exist as such only for our perceptions. Three conclusions, according to Spinoza, follow from this. In the first place, neither can have any originating creative quality about it, and therefore the human will is no freer than inanimate nature from the rule of unalterable law. In the second place we are unable to predicate purpose, or even personality, of God. In the third place the dissolution of the body means the dissolution of the soul, or rather the resolution of individual existence into the one divine substance from which it sprang.

For a long time Western thought was unable to appreciate any religious element in Spinoza's system—that "echo from the East," as it has been well called—and regarded it as equivalent to blank atheism. A century had to elapse before that sentence of his, which Goethe has made famous, "Who truly loves God must not demand that God shall love him in return," could stir a responsive chord in human intelligence. Meantime the Leibnitzian philosophy was created in order, without going back to the old Cartesian antithesis, to find a place for the direct action of the Deity, and for human freedom. To explain the philosophy of Leibnitz is no easy matter. He was one of those supreme thinkers who know that a truth when formulated is a truth no

longer. " His conceptions of truth," said Lessing to
Jacobi in the conversations already mentioned, " were
of such a nature that he could not bear to set too
narrow limits to it. To this habit of thought many of
his assertions are due, and it is often difficult for the
greatest penetration to discover his true meaning. Just
for that do I value him so—I mean for this great manner
of thinking, and not for this or that opinion which
he may, or may seem to, have held." His opinions
were apparently these. Spinoza had defined substance
as that which is *self*-existing : Leibnitz added the predicate of *activity*. The whole universe, like a bent
bow, is ever straining towards action. But this conception of an active force necessarily implies multiplicity.
Such a force must be an excludent force, and there
must be something to exclude. Substance, therefore,
is not only self-existent, but active, not only active, but
multiple, and therefore also individual, for multiplicity
is made up of individuals. These individuals are named
by Leibnitz monads. They are not material atoms, for
matter with Leibnitz is only a confused, subjective
perception, but indivisible centres of living force.
They differ in faculty from each other—indeed none is
regarded as being exactly like another. In those which
compose the world of inorganic nature, consciousness
lies in a trance like death ; in plants it is seen to live and
move ; in animal monads it dreams ; in the human soul
it is awake.

The monads are, by the law of their being, impelled
to constant activity. At the same time Leibnitz was
unable to imagine any principle of interaction among

them ; for all connected things are complementary, and therefore individually deficient, while each monad is to be conceived as a complete entity. How then does it come about that the sum of these infinite unrelated activities produces order and not chaos? The answer is that each monad has perceptions, not only of its own successive states, but also of those of all the other monads. Each is a mirror of the whole universe (though they mirror it in various degrees of distinctness), and its activities are thus harmonized with those of its fellow-beings by perceptions which are common to all. But if harmony follows from these perceptions, the thing perceived must be harmonious. And so Leibnitz concludes that between monad and monad—as, for instance, between the exalted monad which is called the soul and those inferior ones which form the body of any man, there exists a pre-established harmony. Each pursues its own course unaffected by the other, but each is affected by a pre-existent conception of the orderly course of the whole world, just as two clocks of perfect mechanism would strike together for ever if once set to the same time. The author of this cosmic conception is God. This view is then applied by Leibnitz to a question much debated in his day. It is clear that if God, out of the infinite possibilities before Him, chose to conceive the world as we find it, it must be the best of all possible worlds—the best which could be realized according to the given conditions.

If we disregard the famous conversations with Jacobi, there is no doubt that Lessing must be reckoned as in the main a follower of Leibnitz. His "Pope a Metaphysician " is thoroughly Leibnitzian, and in it Spinoza's system is even stigmatized as an "edifice of error," although we know that the sincerity and philosophic spirit of Spinoza had already won his interest and admiration.[1] And to the end of his life there is constant evidence of Lessing's interest in Leibnitz. He had even begun to collect materials for a biography of him. In his discussion of Leibnitz's views on Eternal Punishment, in the Wolfenbüttel Contributions, he protests against the habit of speaking of the doctrine of the best of all possible worlds as the doctrine of *Leibnitz*, as though there were any other which a philosophical thinker could entertain. And the monadology of Leibnitz served him as a point of departure for various speculations, such as that of the transmigration of souls, or the possibility of having more than five senses, to which he could hardly have been led by Spinoza. On the other hand, in the conversations with Jacobi, in which, whatever their value as evidences of Lessing's opinions, it will be obvious to any reader who knows Lessing's style that his utterances are accurately reproduced, he avows himself a thorough Spinozist. ""Εν καὶ πᾶν (One and All)"—a favourite saying of Lessing's in these days—" I know nothing else than that." "I do not want my will to be free." "Extension, Motion, Thought, are obviously grounded in a higher power which is far from being exhausted by them. It must be infinitely superior to this or that operation of it, and so there may be a kind of enjoyment for it which not alone surpasses our conceptions but is absolutely beyond all conception . . . *Jacobi:*

[1] Letter to Michaelis, October 17, 1754.

You go further than Spinoza—he set insight above everything.[1] *Lessing:* Yes, for men. But he was far from
asserting our wretched way of acting according to purposes to be the highest way, and setting Thought above
all." "Leibnitz was at heart a Spinozist." "There is
no other philosophy." Which latter opinion Jacobi
agrees with, but rescues himself from pantheism and
fatalism by a mental somersault, a *salto mortale*, for
which Lessing says his old bones are too stiff.

In the face of evidence like this, taken together with
that of his writings, it seems hard to doubt that Lessing
did really endeavour to combine the primary features of
the Spinozistic system with the monadology of Leibnitz,
interpreting the " harmony " of the monadic universe
by the actual immanence of the Deity, rather than by
an exercise of His will on something external to Him.[2]
But we must beware how we formulate Lessing, just
as Lessing would have us beware how we formulate
Leibnitz. No *intellectual* truth had for him more than
a provisional value—he did not even wish to think that
it had more :—"Not the truth," he wrote in the
Duplik, " not the truth which a man possesses, or thinks
he possesses, but the sincere endeavour which he has
used to come at the truth, makes the worth of the man.

---

[1] The knowledge of God being the highest human bliss.

[2] See a brief note, "On the Reality of Things Outside God,"
published among his posthumous papers. He argues, that such things
have no reality. God's conceptions are creations, they *are* the things
themselves. This idea is applied, in "The Christianity of Reason,"
(a brief treatise published after Lessing's death) to the Christian
doctrine of the Trinity, *e.g.*, God is ever representing Himself to
Himself—as represented, He is the Son, as representing, the Father.

For not through the possession of truth, but through the search for it, are those powers expanded in which alone his ever-growing perfection consists. Possession makes restful, indolent, proud——

"If God were to hold in His right hand all truth, and in His left the single ever-living impulse to seek for truth, though coupled with the condition of eternal error, and should say to me, 'Choose!' I would humbly fall before His left hand, and say, 'Father, give! Pure truth is, after all, for Thee alone.'" [1]

There is nothing in Lessing more characteristic than this striking utterance. His ethics were those of Stoicism; based, not on any ultra-mundane hypotheses, but on a large and reverent interpretation of human experience. And on the speculative side, too, he confronted the universe in the spirit of antique philosophy—a spirit of cheerful exploration, of eager yet unanxious inquiry. He looked forward to the future life as calmly as to an earthly morrow, not because he knew what it would bring him, but because he was as well content with God's darkness as with His light.

---

[1] "Malebranche disait avec une ingénieuse exagération 'Si je tenais la vérité captive dans ma main, j'ouvrirais la main afin de poursuivre encore la vérité.'" Mazure, "Cours de la Philosophie," t. ij. p. 20. See Sir W. Hamilton, "Lectures on Metaph.," i. 13.

CHAPTER XVIII

JACOBI and his sister Helene left Wolfenbüttel on July 9, 1780, accompanied by Lessing as far as Brunswick, where the latter spent some days. On August 10th Jacobi returned to Brunswick, where he was joined by Lessing, and the next day they started to Halberstadt, to pay a visit to the hospitable Gleim—a pleasant journey brightened by much cheerful talk. The pleasure derived from the sight of a beautiful landscape was a subject which naturally suggested itself. Lessing admitted that he was not wholly insensible to this pleasure. " I like this better than the Lüneberger Haide ; but even the Lüneberger Haide I could endure much better than a room whose walls are not set square. In such a room I simply cannot live." Gleim received his visitors with his usual friendliness. He noticed that Lessing was sometimes overcome with his tendency to drowsiness, which had much increased of late, and that he and Jacobi constantly led the conversation to Spinoza and his doctrines. In Gleim's summer-house, where many distinguished authors had inscribed their names, Lessing appended to his own his favourite Ἓν καὶ πᾶν, together with a Latin sentence, *Dies in lite* (A day of strife).

Four days Lessing and Jacobi remained at Halberstadt. "This little trip has done me a world of good," he wrote to Malchen; nothing, indeed, ever did him more good than to escape from the loneliness of Wolfenbüttel to the cheerful society of his peers. He now, however, settled down at Wolfenbüttel to finish his "Letters to Various Theologians," and to prepare a fifth "Contribution," which should be chiefly concerned with the subject in which he had all his life taken such interest—the Fable.

But quiet and steady work in the solitude of Wolfenbüttel was no longer possible to him, and his restlessness soon drove him out into the world again. This time he went to Hamburg (Oct. 9), and with the best results for his health and spirits. So capable of work did he soon feel himself again that he even promised the Hamburg Theatre a new play by the end of the year, for which he was to receive one hundred ducats. No representation of "Nathan" could be thought of, but he had the pleasure of hearing his drama well read in a private assembly, the accomplished actor Schröder taking the parts of Nathan and the Patriarch.

He returned to Brunswick on November 1st, mentally and physically the better for his change, but there the clouds soon closed in again.

"Quickly as I hurried home," he wrote to Elise, "I was sorry to arrive, for the first thing I found was myself. And in this discontent with myself can I begin to be healthy and do my work? 'Surely,' I hear my friends call after me; 'for a man like you can

do anything that he will.' But, dear friends, does that mean anything else than 'can do what he can?' And if I shall ever again
feel this *can*—that, indeed, is the question. But what can be done
without trying? Well, then, my dear friend, since you too advise
it, so let it be."

He now pushed his fifth "Contribution" in some
degree forward, and thought of redeeming his promise
to the Hamburg Theatre by an adaptation of the
"London Prodigal," one of the plays of unknown
authorship sometimes attributed to Shakspere.

Towards the middle of November he visited Brunswick, and on the 22nd spent a pleasant evening with
Leisewitz, and other literary friends, in the club which
these congenial spirits had founded there. "We were
in high spirits," reports Leisewitz in his diary, "sub-
tilized, laughed, philosophized, sentimentalized, and
combined these two latter things in a discourse on love."

The following day Lessing received a summons from
the Duke. The latter had a very serious communication
to make. He had received private information that the
Protestant Estates of the Empire had resolved to
summon him, the Duke, to inflict due punishment on
the editor of the last scandalous Fragment—"On the
Aims of Jesus and His Disciples." The manner in
which he conveyed this news was so friendly, and
his resolve to stand by Lessing so clear, that the
latter afterwards regretted the churlish indifference with
which he bade the Duke act on his ministers' advice,
and leave him to fight his own battles. "After all," he
said, "he has a noble nature; I know not why I have
been so out of temper with him lately." The Duke

however, did not take Lessing's conduct in bad part, attributing it probably to its true cause—the irritability and depression of his illness.

Whether the Protestant Estates saw that Lessing's position, as the mere editor of the Fragments, was impregnable ; or that to summon the Duke of Brunswick, a known champion of religious liberty, to punish his librarian, was not a very hopeful course, the project fell to the ground; but it must have caused Lessing, who was little fitted for a new struggle, much annoyance and anxiety. Largely as Semler had undermined the old convictions of Protestantism, the Fragments, with their sincerity and thoroughness, had brought about a temporary reaction of feeling, some of whose symptoms Lessing had to observe with much disgust. In the Duchy of Jülich-Berg it had lately been decreed that absence from church and the Holy Communion should be punished with a fine, or, if persistent, with imprisonment and banishment. " Heavens ! the scoundrels ! " wrote Lessing to Jacobi. "They deserve to be again oppressed by the Papacy, and to become the slaves of a cruel Inquisition."

In December he again visited Brunswick, and his friends noticed a serious change in his condition. Every breath was laboured, his gait was feeble, the "tiger-eyes " were now dull and often almost sightless, in conversation he was absent and forgetful ; too plainly did he feel

> " The senses break away
> To mix with ancient Night."

But the heart, where is man's life of life, felt no chill

from the approaching end, and there is something profoundly touching in the cry of love and sadness with which he turns to his old friend Mendelssohn, on whose last letter of praise and thanks for some late "printed evidences of his continued existence" he was still feeding :—

"I much need such a letter from time to time, if I am not to become utterly dejected. I think you know me for a man who is not greedy of praise. But the coldness with which the world is wont to assure certain people that they can do nothing that is right in its eyes, is, if not deadly, at least benumbing. That you are not pleased with everything I have lately written, I do not wonder. Nothing should have pleased you, for nothing was written for you. At most, you may have been beguiled here and there by the remembrance of our better days. I, too, was then a healthy and slender sapling, and am now such a gnarled and rotten trunk ! Ah, dear friend, this scene is over. But I wish I could speak with you once again !" [1]

The weather grew gloomy and cold as the new year set in, and Lessing's eyes suffered severely from it. He could not for four weeks send to his friends in Hamburg the weekly report of his health which he had promised them. But at last some sunny days came, and he wrote to Elise, who had anxiously begged for news :—

"I have indeed, my love, been ill again. If I were *only* busy, would that have kept me from writing to you ?—And more ill than ever. Not that my head is still lodging in my stomach—thanks to your brother's pills ; but my eyes are lodging there, and I am as good as blind. . . . But I am writing to you, you will say ; it is a wonderfully bright day, and I have a splendid new pair of spectacles. Your brother will remember that I complained to him

---

[1] Lessing's last letter to Mendelssohn, December 19, 1780.

about my eyes ten years ago. . . . I cannot now remember what made me better then. Perhaps I only learned to adapt myself to my misfortune, which at that time was not very great. My God ! if that should ever be so again ! And if you really knew how long I have been writing this letter ! "

Towards the end of January things were so far improved with him that he could leave Wolfenbüttel, and he went to Brunswick for the Fair, which began there on February 5th. One day he dined with the Duke, and spent the afternoon at the club, where Leisewitz showed him a defence of German literature, written by the Abbot Jerusalem, in reply to certain recent ignorant criticisms of Frederick the Great. Jerusalem had rested his case largely on the merits of Winckelmann and Lessing. In the evening he was the guest of the Dowager Duchess, and afterwards looked in at the Davesons. Here he was seized with a violent asthmatic attack. They brought him to his own lodgings, where he passed a very restless night. Next day he felt so much better that he wished to return to Wolfenbüttel, but the Court physician, whom they had prevailed upon him to consult, forbade it, and Malchen was at once summoned. The disease was dropsy of the chest, accompanied with inflammation of the lungs and intestines.

He sometimes felt so comparatively well that he doubted if the end were actually at hand, but he declared himself prepared for either death or life, and awaited the decision of fate. " He died like a sage," it was said of him, and, indeed, a certain Socratic calm and cheerfulness marked these last days. His friends,

Daveson, Leisewitz, and others, were constantly with him, and he enjoyed their company. When too tired for conversation he would have them read aloud to him. Among others the Abbot Jerusalem visited him, but was not admitted till Lessing was assured that he did not come

> "To canvass with official breath
> The future and its viewless things."

On the 15th the load of his illness was markedly lightened; he rose from bed and talked with much of his old vivacity. In the evening, while in his bedroom, he was told that a new visitor had just arrived to see him. He rose, opened the door which led into the adjoining room, and stood before them; but his strength was exhausted and he could not speak. Malchen was sitting by the door, her face turned away so that he might not see her tears. He turned upon her a silent look of tenderness and pity, then his limbs failed, and he was carried back to bed. A painful attack of asthma followed. It was the last. A few minutes afterwards, while lying in the arms of Daveson, who was reading aloud to him, they perceived that "all was dead of him that here can die."

"We lose much, much, in him; more than we think," wrote Goethe to Frau Stein. But his work was done—and what a work! It is true that he dwelt no long time in any of the many regions which he traversed. But wherever his foot fell it left an ineffaceable trace, even such as those

> "mighty footprints that report
> The giant form of antique Literature."

No question left his hands without having been visibly advanced; and wherever he laboured he laboured with the noble strenuousness and piety of one to whom every place is sacred that Truth inhabits. We may well say of him as he said of Leibnitz, that his great manner of thinking, apart from the positive conclusions he supported, would alone have been an influence of the deepest value for his day and land.

His outward life has often been regarded as one of the many examples of the misery and ill success which attend genius. And certainly it had great sorrows, privations, and disappointments, which he felt to the full. But if he had much to bear, he had a very stout heart wherewith to bear it. A manlier character there is not in the whole history of literature. And he knew how to turn his sorrow into labour, to dull the sense of earthly losses by the pursuit of ideal aims. Nor was his life by any means made up of losses and disappointments. He loved battle, and he had many battles, and was victorious in every one of them. He loved friendship, and no man had ever warmer and worthier friends. He had fame, if he cared for that; and before his death he had what he certainly did care for—the sight of a new generation, full of buoyancy, genius, and hope, addressing itself to the tasks to which he had summoned it. He was no self-pitier; and not with pity, but rather with proud congratulation, let us leave the stalwart fighter in the arms of Honour, Love, and Death.

THE END.

INDEX.

---

[1] The note on p. 91 founded on Düntzer's *Leben* (*see* Index, Gottlob. S. Nicolai and reference, p. 240) is incorrect. The Frankfurt Professor was identical with Lange's friend.

BIBLIOGRAPHY.

BY

JOHN P. ANDERSON

(British Museum).

I. WORKS.

G. E. Lessing's Schriften. 6 Thle. Berlin, 1753-55, 12mo.

G. E. Lessing's sämmtliche Schriften. 30 Thle. 1771-94, 8vo.

G. E. Lessing's sämmtliche Werke. 30 Thle. Carlsruhe, 1824-25, 12mo.

G. E. Lessing's sämmtliche Schriften. [Edited, with a Life of Lessing, by J. F. Schink, and additions by J. J. Eschenburg.] 32 Bde. Berlin, 1825-28, 8vo.

G. E. Lessing's sämmtliche Schriften, herausgegeben von K. Lachmann. 13 Bde. Berlin, 1838-40, 8vo.

Werke. Ausgabe in 8 Banden. Berlin, 1840, 12mo.

Lessing's sämmtliche Werke in einem Bande. Mit dem Bildniss des Verfassers. Leipzig, 1841, 8vo.

Gesammelte Werke. Neue rechtmässige Ausgabe. 10 Bde. Leipzig, 1841, 16mo.

G. E. Lessing's sämmtliche Schriften. Herausgegeben von K. Lachmann. Auf's Neue durchgesehen und vermehrt von W. von Maltzahn. 12 Bde. Leipzig, 1853-57, 8vo.

G. E. Lessing's gesammelte Werke. 2 Bde. Leipzig, 1859, 8vo.

Lessing's Werke in 6 Bdn. Stuttgart, 1869, 16mo.

Lessing's Werke. Herausgegeben
von Richard Gosche. Erste
illustrirte Ausgabe. 54 Lfgn.
Berlin, 1875-6, 8vo.
Lessing's Werke. Nebst Biographie des Dichters. (Thl. 7,
Hamburgische Dramaturgie.
Einleitung des Herausgebers G.
Zimmermann. Thl. 8, heraus-
gegeben mit Anmerkungen von
R. Pilger. Thl. 9, 10, 12, 19,
20, von C. C. Redlich. Thl.
13, von E. Grosse. Thl. 14-18,
von C. Gross.) 20 Thle. Ber-
lin [1879], 8vo.
Lessing's Briefe. Nachträge und
Berichtigungen [to Abth. 1 and
2, Th. xx. of "Lessing's
Werke," edited in part by C.
C. Redlich]. Herausgegeben
und mit Anmerkungen be-
gleitet von C. C. Redlich. Ber-
lin, 1886, 8vo.
Lessing's Werke. [Edited by
H. Laube.] 5 Bde. Leipzig
[1881-3], 8vo.
Lessing's sämmtliche Werke.
Herausgegeben von R. Gosche.
(1, 3, 5-8 Bde. bearbeitet von
R. Boxberger; Bd. 2, 4, von R.
Gosche, etc.) 8 Bde. Berlin,
1882, 8vo.
Lessing's Werke. Neu heraus-
gegeben von F. Bornmüller.
5 Bde. Leipzig, 1884, 8vo.
G. E. Lessing's Gesammelte
Werke. Mit einer literarhis-
torisch - biographischen Ein-
leitung von M. Koch. 3 Bde.
Stuttgart, 1886, 8vo.

Lessing's Dramen und dramatische Fragmente. Zum Ersten-
male vollständig erläutert von
A. Nodnagel. Supplement-
band zu sämmtlichen Ausgaben von Lessing's Werken.
Darmstadt, 1842, 8vo.

Poetische und dramatische Werke.
Leipzig, 1867, 16mo.
Sämmtliche lyrische, epische und
dramatische Werke, und seine
vorzüglichen Prosaschriften.
Teschen, 1868, 8vo.
Poetische und dramatische Werke,
etc. Stuttgart [1869], 16mo.
   Forming part of "Göpel's Illus-
trirte Classiker Ausgaben."
G. E. Lessing's schönwissen-
schaftliche Schriften. 7 Bände.
Berlin, 1827, 12mo.
Auswahl von Lessing's Werken.
5 Thle. Gotha, 1827, 16mo.
   Vol. xi. of the "Miniatur-
Bibliothek der deutschen Classiker."
The Dramatic Works of G. E.
Lessing. Translated from the
German. Edited by Ernest Bell.
With a short memoir by Helen
Zimmern. 2 vols. London,
1878, 8vo.
   Part of Bohn's "Standard
Library."
Selected Prose Works of G. E.
Lessing, translated from the
German by E. C. Beasley and
Helen Zimmern. Edited by
Edward Bell. London, 1879,
8vo.
   Part of "Bohn's Standard
brary."
Three Comedies (Der Freigeist—
Der Schatz—Minna von Barn-
helm). Translated from the
German by J. J. Holroyd.
Colchester, 1838, 8vo.

Die Alte Jungfer. Ein Lustspiel
in drey Aufzügen. Berlin,
1749, 8vo.
Anti-Goeze. 11 Stücke. Braunschweig, 1778, 8vo.
Nöthige Antwort auf eine
unnöthige Frage des Herrn
Pastor Götze in Hamburg.
Leipzig, 1778, 8vo.

Axiomata, wenn es deren in dergleichen Dingen giebt. Braunschweig, 1778, 8vo.

Beiträge zur Historie und Aufnahme des Theaters. 4 Stück. Stargard, 1750, 8vo.

Berengarius Turonensis: oder, Ankündigung eines wichtigen Werkes desselben, etc. Braunschweig, 1770, 4to.

Beschreibung des Portugiesischen Amerika vom Cudena. Ein Spanisches Manuscript in der Wolfenbüttelschen Bibliothek, herausgegeben vom Herrn Hofrath Lessing. Braunschweig, 1780, 8vo.

Uber den Beweis des Geistes und der Kraft, etc. Braunschweig, 1777, 8vo.

Briefe antiquarischen Inhalts. 2 Thle. Berlin, 1768, 8vo.

Emilia Galotti. Ein Trauerspiel in fünf Aufzügen. Berlin, 1772, 8vo.

——Emilia Galotti : a tragedy in five acts. Translated by Fanny Holcroft. (*The Theatrical Recorder*, vol. i., 1805, pp. 363-409.)

Eine ernsthafte Ermunterung an alle Christen zu einem frommen und heiligen Leben. Von William Law. Aus dem Englischen übersetzt. Leipzig, 1756, 8vo.

Ernst und Falk. Gespräch für Freimäurer. Wolfenbüttel, 1778, 8vo.

Die Erziehung des Menschengeschlechts. Herausgegeben von G. E. Lessing. Berlin, 1780, 8vo.

——The Education of the Human Race. From the German of G. E. Lessing [by F. W. Robertson]. London, 1858, 8vo.

——Third edition, London, 1872, 16mo.

G. E. Lessing's Fabeln nebst Abhandlungen mit dieser Dichtungsart verwandten Inhalts. Berlin, 1759, 8vo.

——Lessing's Fables. In three books. *Ger.* and *Eng.* London, 1829, 12mo.

——Fables from the German. Translated by J. Richardson. York, 1773, 8vo.

——Fables and Epigrams ; with Essays on Fable and Epigram. From the German of Lessing. London, 1825, 8vo.

——Fables and Parables from the German of Lessing, Herder (Krummacher and others). London [1845], 12mo. Part of "Burns' Fireside Library.'

——Lessing's German Fables in prose and verse. With a close English translation and brief notes. London, 1860, 8vo.

——Lessing's Fables. Edited, with notes, by F. Storr. London, 1878, 8vo.

Fragmente des Wolfenbüttel'schen Ungenannten. Anhang zu dem Fragmente vom Zwecke Jesu und seiner Jünger [by Samuel Reimarus], bekannt gemacht von Lessing. Berlin, 1784, 8vo.

Fragments from Reimarus, consisting of brief critical remarks on the object of Jesus and his disciples, as seen by the New Testament. Translated from the German of G. E. Lessing. London, 1879, 8vo.

Eine Duplik. [A reply to the "Fragmente und Antifragmente" of J. C. Doederlein.] Braunschweig, 1778, 8vo.

Franz Hutchisons der Rechte Doctors und der Weltweisheit Professors zu Glasgow Sittenlehre der Vernunft, aus dem

Englischen übersetzt. 2 Bde. Leipzig, 1756, 8vo.

Die Gefangnen. Ein Lustspiel. Aus dem Lateinischen des M. Accius Plautus übersetzt. Stuttgard, 1750, 8vo.

Hamburgische Dramaturgie. 2 Bde. Hamburg [1769], 8vo.

Johann Huart's Prüfung der Köpfe zu den Wissenschaften. Aus dem Spanischen übersetzt von G. E. Lessing. Zerbst, 1752, 8vo.

Der Junge Gelehrte in der Einbildung, ein Lustspiel in drey Aufzügen. Wein [1764], 8vo.

Kleinigkeiten. Frankfurt, 1751, 8vo.

Laokoon; oder über die Grenzen der Mahlerey und Poesie; mit beyläufigen Erläuterungen verschiedener Punkte der alten Kunstgeschichte. Thl. I. Berlin, 1766, 8vo.
  No more published.

——Neue vermehrte Auflage herausgegeben von K. G. Lessing. Berlin, 1788, 8vo.

——Laocoon; or, the Limits of Poetry and Painting. Translated from the German of G. E. Lessing by W. Ross. London, 1836, 8vo.

——Laocoon: an Essay on the Limits of Painting and Poetry. Translated from the German by E. C. Beasley. With an Introduction by T. Burbridge. London, 1853, 8vo.

——Laocoon; an Essay upon the Limits of Painting and Poetry. Translated by E. Frothingham. Boston, 1874, 8vo.

——Laocoon. Translated from the text of Lessing, with preface and notes, by Sir R. Phillimore. With illustrations. London, 1874, 8vo.

——Lessing's Laokoon. Translated from the German by E. C. Beasley. London, 1888, 8vo.
  Part of "Bohn's Shilling Library."

Gotthold Ephraim Lessing's Kollektaneen zur Literatur. Herausgegeben von J. J. Eschenburg. 2 Bde. Berlin, 1790, 8vo.

G. E. Lessing's Leben des Sophocles. Herausgegeben von J. J. Eschenburg. Berlin, 1790, 8vo.

Lustspiele. 2 Thle. Berlin, 1767, 8vo.

F. von Logau. Sinngedichte. Herausgegeben von C. W. Ramler und G. E. Lessing. Leipzig, 1759, 8vo.

Minna von Barnhelm, oder das Soldatenglück. Ein Lustspiel in 5 Aufzügen. Berlin, 1767, 8vo.

——The School for Honour; or, The Chance of War: a comedy in five acts. Translated from the German of Lessing. London, 1799, 8vo.

——The Disbanded Officer; or, The Baroness of Bruchsal: a comedy (altered from "Minna von Barnhelm," by J. J. Johnstone]. London, 1786, 8vo.

——Minna von Barnhelm; a comedy in five acts. Translated by Fanny Holcroft. (*The Theatrical Recorder*, vol. ii., 1806, pp. 213-260.)

——Minna von Barnhelm; or, a Soldier's Fortune. A comedy in five acts, from the German. Translated into English, together with notes in German, by W. E. Wrankmore. Leipzig, 1858, 8vo.

Der Misogyne, oder der Feind des weiblichen Geschlechts. Ein Lustspiel in zwey Aufzügen. Wien, 1762, 8vo.

G. E. Lessing's Nachlass zur deutschen Sprache, alten Literatur, Gelehrten-und Kunstgeschichte. Geordnet von G. G. Fülleborn. Berlin, 1795, 8vo.

Nathan der Weise. Ein dramatisches Gedicht, in fünf Aufzügen. [Berlin] 1779, 8vo.

——Nathan the Wise; a philosophical drama [in five acts and in prose]. Translated by R. E. Raspe. London, 1781, 8vo.

——Nathan the Wise. A dramatic poem, written originally in German, etc. [Translated into English verse by William Taylor, of Norwich.] Norwich, 1791, 8vo.

——Nathan the Wise. A dramatic poem, in five acts. Translated from the German, with a biography of Lessing, and a critical survey of his position, by A. Reich. London, 1860, 12mo.

——Nathan the Wise. Translated by W. Taylor.—Emilia Galotti. Translated by C. L. Lewes. Leipzig, 1868, 8vo.
Vol. ix. of the " Tauchnitz Collection of German Authors."

——Nathan the Wise; a dramatic poem. [Translated] from the German. With an introduction on Lessing and the "Nathan;" its antecedents, character, and influence [signed R. W., M.D., i.e., Robert Willis]. London, 1868. 8vo.

——Nathan the Wise. Translated by E. Frothingham. Preceded by a brief account of the poet and his works [signed H. H.], and followed by K. Fischer's essay on the Poem.

Second edition, revised. New York, 1868, 12mo.

——Nathan the Wise. A drama in five acts. Abridged and translated from the German [into English prose], by E. S. H. London, 1874, 4to.

——Nathan the Wise. A dramatic poem; translated into English verse by Andrew Wood. London, 1877, 8vo.

——Lessing's Nathan the Wise; translated into English verse by E. K. Corbett, with an introduction and notes. London, 1883, 8vo.

——Nathan the Wise. Translated by William Taylor, of Norwich. London, 1886, 8vo.
Vol. 38 of "Cassell's National Library."

Eine Parabel. Nebst einer kleinen Bitte, und einem eventualen Absagungsschreiben an den Herrn Pastor Goeze, in Hamburg. [A reply, by G. E. Lessing, to Goetze's criticisms, entitled "Freiwillige Beiträge," etc.] Braunschweig, 1778, 8vo.

Philosophische Aufsätze von Karl Wilhelm Jerusalem, herausgegeben von G. E. Lessing. Braunschweig, 1776, 8vo.

Philotas. Ein Trauerspiel. Berlin, 1759, 8vo.

Preussische Kriegslieder in den Feldzügen 1756 und 1757 von einem Grenadier. [With a preface by G. E. Lessing.] Berlin [1758], 16mo.

Miss Sara Sampson. Berlin, 1772, 8vo.

Schreiben an das Publicum. Aus dem Französischen, i.-iii. Berlin, 1753, 8vo.

Der Schatz, Lustspiel in einem Aufzuge. Paderborn, 1877, 8vo.

Hrn. Samuel Richardsons, Verfassers der Pamela, der Clarissa
und des Grandisons Sittenlehre
für die Jugend in den auserles-
ensten Aesopischen Fabeln, etc.
Leipzig, 1757, 8vo. '

Römische Historie von Erbauung
der Stadt Rom bis auf die
Schlacht bey Actium, oder das
Ende der Republik ; aus dem
Französichen des Herrn Rollins.
Thl. 4-6. Leipzig, 1749-1752,
8vo.

Das Testament Johannis, ein
Gespräch. Braunschweig, 1777,
8vo.

Das Theater des Herrn Diderot.
Aus dem Französischen [by G.
E. Lessing]. 2 Thle. Berlin,
1760, 12mo.

G. E. Lessing's Theatralische
Bibliothek. 4 St. Berlin,
1754-58, 8vo.

G. E. Lessing's Theatralischer
Nachlass. [Edited by C. G.
Lessing.] 2 Thle. Berlin,
1784-86, 8vo.

G. E. Lessing's theologischer
Nachlass. [Edited by C. G.
Lessing.] Berlin, 1784, 8vo.

Des Herrn Jacob Thomson sämmtliche Trauerspiele. Aus dem
Englischen übersetzt. Leipzig,
1754, 8vo.

Trauerspiele. Berlin, 1772, 8vo.

Ein Vade Mecum für den Herrn
S. G. Lange, Pastor in Lam-
blingen. Berlin, 1754, 12mo.

Vermischte Schriften des Hrn.
Christlob Mylius, gesammelt
von G. E. Lessing. Berlin,
1754, 8vo.

Vom Alter der Oelmalerey, aus
dem Theophilus Presbyter.
Braunschweig, 1774, 8vo.

Von dem Zwecke Jesu und seiner
Jünger. Herausgegeben von G.
E. Lessing. Berlin, 1778, 8vo.

Wie die Alten den Tod gebildet :
eine Untersuchung. Berlin,
1769, 4to.

Zur Geschichte und Litteratur.
Aus den Schätzen der Herzog-
lichen Bibliothek zu Wolfenbüttel. [Beytrag 5, by G. E.
Lessing and J. J. Eschenburg.
Beytrag 6, edited by C. Leiste.]
3 vols. Braunschweig, 1773-81,
8vo.

II. LETTERS.

Briefwechsel mit seinem Bruder
K. G. Lessing, herausgegeben
von K. G. Lessing. Berlin,
1795, 8vo.

Briefwechsel mit Fr. W. Gleim
1757-1779. Berlin, 1795, 8vo.

Briefwechsel zwischen Lessing
und seiner Frau, neu herausgegeben von Dr. A. Schöne,
nebst einem Anhang bisher
ungedruckter Briefe. Mit dem
Portrait von Frau Lessing.
Leipzig, 1870, 8vo.

Freundschaftlicher Briefwechsel
zwischen G. E. Lessing und
seiner Frau, herausgegeben von
K. G. Lessing. 2 Thle. Berlin,
1789, 8vo.

Gelehrter Briefwechsel zwischen
ihm, J. J. Reiske und Moses
Mendelssohn. Herausgegeben
von K. G. Lessing. 2 Thle.
Berlin, 1789, 8vo.

——Gelehrter Briefwechsel zwisch-
en J. J. Reiske, Moses Mendelssohn, und G. E. Lessing.
Ofen, 1820, 12mo.
Bd. 9 of "Moses Mendelssohn's
sämmtliche Werke."

III. SELECTIONS.

Aphorismen aus Lessing's hamburgischer Dramaturgie, zusam-

mengestellt von H. Ziegler. Erfurt, 1882, 8vo.

Lessing's Geist aus seinen Schriften, oder dessen Gedanken und Meinungen zusammengestellt und erläutert von F. Schlegel. 3 Thle. Leipzig, 1810, 8vo.

G. E. Lessing. Lichtstrahlen aus seinen Schriften und Briefen. Mit einer Einleitung von F. Bloemer. Leipzig, 1869, 8vo.

IV. APPENDIX.

BIOGRAPHY, CRITICISM, ETC.

Albrecht, Friedrich.—Moses Mendelssohn als Urbild von Lessing's Nathan dem Weisen. Ulm [1866], 8vo.

Auerbach, Berthold.—Epilog zur Lessing-Feier nach der Aufführung von Emilie Galotti im Hoftheater zu Dresden, gesprochen von Emil Devrient am 16 Marz 1850. Dresden, 1850, 8vo.

——Die Genesis des Nathan. Berlin, 1881, 8vo.

Back, Samuel.—Das Synhedrion unter Napoleon I., etc. Vortrag zum hundertjährigen Jubiläum des Lessing'schen " Nathan." Prag, 1879, 8vo.

Bärthold, Albert.—Lessing und die objective Wahrheit, aus Sören Kierkegaards Schriften zusammengestellt. Halle, 1877, 8vo.

Bauer, Edgard—Gotthold Ephraim Lessing als Ordensbruder. (*Zwei Ordenskizzen*, No. ii.) Leipzig, 1881, 8vo.

Baumgart, Hermann—Aristoteles, Lessing, und Goethe. Ueber

des ethische und das aesthetische Princip der Tragödie. Leipzig, 1877, 8vo.

Beck, Ernst.—Das Lessingfest zu Kamenz am 1 Juni 1863. Kamenz [1863], 8vo.

Becker, *Pastor*.—Johann Melchior Goeze und Lessing, etc.—Flensburg, 1887, 8vo.

Belmont, *pseud* [*i.e.*, H. A. Schuemberg].—Den Manen G. E. Lessings. Beschreibung der am Secular-Geburtsfeste der Gefeierten in seiner Vaterstadt Camenz veranstalteten Feierlichkeiten. Camenz [1829], 8vo.

Benfey, R.— Lessing die Grundsäule deutscher Literatur. (*Aus der Liturgeschichte für's Volk*, Hft. i.) Berlin, 1868, 8vo.

Bergmann, E. A. — Hermaea. Studien zu G. E. Lessings theologischen und philosophischen Schriften. Leipzig, 1883, 8vo.

Beyschlag, W.—Lessing's Nathan der Weise und das positive Christenthum. Berlin [1863], 8vo.

Bloch, J. S.—Quellen und Parallelen zu Lessing's " Nathan," etc. Wien, 1880, 8vo.

Bloemer, Friedrich. — Lessing, Schiller, und Goethe, etc. Berlin, 1863, 8vo.

Boden, August.— Lessing und Goeze. Ein Beitrag zur Literatur-und Kirchengeschichte des achtzehnten Jahrhunderts, etc. Leipzig, 1862, 8vo.

——Ueber die Echtheit und den Werth der " Zu Lessings Andenken," durch W. Wattenbach herausgegebenen Briefe, etc. Leipzig, 1863, 8vo.

Bodmer, J. J.— Polytimet, ein Trauerspiel. Parodie des Philotas. Zürich, 1870, 8vo.

Bohtz, A. W.—G. E. Lessing's Protestantismus und Nathan der Weise. Göttingen, 1854, 8vo.

Borgius, E.—Lessing's Nathan und der Mönch vom Libanon (von J. G. Pfranger). Barmen [1881], 8vo.

Bossert, A.—Goethe, ses précurseurs et ses contemporains, Klopstock, Lessing, etc. Paris, 1872, 8vo.

——Deuxième édition. Paris, 1882, 8vo.

Böttiger, C. A.—Ilithyia. Ein archäologisches Fragment nach Lessing. Weimar, 1799, 8vo.

Brenning, Emil.—Lessing als Dramatiker und Lessing's Nathan der Weise. Bremen, 1878, 8vo.

Caro, J.—Lessing und Swift. Eine Studie über "Nathan der Weise." Jena, 1869, 8vo.

Carriere, Moriz.—Lessing, Schiller, Goethe, Jean Paul. Giessen, 1862, 8vo.

Cassan, C.—Lessing, Goethe, und Schubart. Studien von C. Cassan. (*Pädagogische Sammelmappe*, Heft. 37.) Leipzig, 1880, 8vo.

Cauer, Edward.—Zum Andenken an G. E. Lessing. Berlin, 1881, 8vo.

Claassen, Johannes.—G. E. Lessings Leben und ausgewählte Werke im Lichte der christlichen Wahrheit. 2 Bde. Gütersloh, 1881, 8vo.

Cosack, Wilhelm.—Materialien zu G. E. Lessing's Hamburgischer Dramaturgie, etc. Paderborn, 1876, 8vo.

Cropp, Johannes.—Lessing's Streit mit Hauptpastor Goeze. Berlin, 1881, 8vo.
  Hft. 155 of the "Deutsche Zeit- und-Streit Fragen."

Crouslé, L.—Lessing et le Gout Français en Allemagne. Paris, 1863, 8vo.

Danzel, T. W.—Gotthold Ephraim Lessing, sein Leben und seine Werke. 2 Bde. Leipzig, 1850-54, 8vo.

——Zweite berichtigte und vermehrte Auflage. 2 Bde. Berlin, 1880-81, 8vo.

Davésiés de Pontès, L.—Poets and Poetry of Germany, biographical and critical notices. 2 vols. London, 1858, 8vo.
  Lessing, vol. ii., pp. 51-104.

Dederich, Hermann.—Gotthold Ephraim Lessing der Apostel der Denkfreiheit, etc. Leipzig [1881], 8vo.

De Quincey, Thomas.—Works. 16 vols. London, 1853-60, 8vo.
  Lessing, vol. xii., pp. 230-303.

Diekmann, E.—Lessing als Theologe. Zürich, 1880, 8vo.

Diller, E. A.—Erinnerungen an G. E. Lessing, etc. Meissen, 1841, 8vo.

Dittmar, Louise.—Lessing und Feuerbach, oder Auswahl aus G. E. Lessing's theologischen Schriften, etc. Offenbach, 1847, 8vo.

Doederlein, J. C.—Fragmente und Antifragmente. Zwey Fragmente eines Ungenannten aus Herrn Lessing's Beyträgen zur Litteratur abgedruckt mit Betrachtungen [by J. C. Doederlein] darüber. 2 Thle. Nürnberg, 1778, 1779, 8vo.

Doering, H.—G. E. Lessing's Biographie. Jena, 1853, 8vo.

Dühring, Eugen.—Die Ueberschätzung Lessing's und dessen Anwaltschaft für die Juden. Karlsruhe, 1881, 8vo.

Die Hinrichtung des "Juden-heiligen," G. E. Lessing durch Dr. E. Dühring. [An answer to the preceding.] Bregenz a. Bodensee, 1881, 8vo.

Düntzer, Heinrich. — Göthe's Faust. Nebst Anhängen über Byron's Manfred und Lessing's Doktor Faust. Köln, 1836, 12mo.

——Lessing's Nathan der Weise. Erläutert von H. Dü zer. Wenigen-Jena, 1863, 8vo.

——Lessing's Leben. Leipzig, 1882, 8vo.

Eckardt, L.—Lessing und das erste deutsche Nationaltheater in Hamburg. Hamburg, 1864, 8vo.

Findel, J. G.—Lessing's Ansichten über Frei-Maurerei, etc. Leipzig, 1881, 8vo.

Fisch, Richard.—Generalmajor v. Stille und Friedrich der Grosse contra Lessing. Berlin, 1885, 8vo.

Fischer, Kuno.—Lessing's Nathan der Weise. Die Idee und die Charaktere der Dichtung dargestellt von K. Fischer. Stuttgart, 1864, 8vo.

——G. E. Lessing als Reformator der deutschen Literatur dargestellt. 2 Thle. Stuttgart, 1881, 8vo.

Fleischer, A. S.—Betrachtungen über Lessing's Bruckstücke, den Horus und die Briefe über die Bibel im Volkston, allen gelehrten Schriftstellern und Bucherrecensenten zu einem Probirstein, etc. Wien, 1787, 8vo.

Fontanès, Ernest.—Le Christianisme Moderne; étude sur Lessing. Paris, 1867, 8vo.

Fuerst, Julius.—Lessing's Nathan der Weise. Historisch und philosophisch erläutert. Leipzig, 1881, 8vo.

Galotti, Emilia.—Ueber einige Schönheiten der Emilia Galotti, etc. Leipzig, 1773, 8vo.

Genée, Rudolph. — Klassische Frauenbilder. Aus dramatischen Dichtungen von Shakespeare, Lessing, etc. Berlin, 1884, 8vo.

Gerhard, C. J. P.—Lessing und Christus. Ein Friedenswort an Israel. Breslau, 1881, 8vo.

Giesse, W. — G. E. Lessing's Nathan der Weise. Darmstadt, 1866, 12mo.

Gostwick, Joseph.—German Culture and Christianity. London, 1882, 8vo.
Lessing, pp. 64-87.

Gotschlich, Emil.—Lessing's Aristotelische Studien und der Einfluss derselben auf seine Werke. Berlin, 1876, 8vo.

Götz, F. — Geliebte Schatten. Bildnisse und Autographen von Klopstock, Wieland, Herder, Lessing, etc. Mannheim, 1858, 4to.

Gräve, H. G.—G. E. Lessing's Lebensgeschichte. Leipzig, 1829, 8vo.

Gravemann, J. F. F.—Ueber die Gründe, mit denen Lessing in seinem Laokoon zu beweisen sucht, dass bei den Griechen das Princip der Kunst die Schönheit gewesen, etc. Rostock, 1867, 8vo.

Grossmann, G. L. — Lessing's Denkmal, etc. Hannover, 1791, 8vo.

Grousilliers, H. de.—Nathan der Weise und die Antisemiten-Liga. Berlin, 1880, 8vo.

Guhrauer, G. E.—Lessing's Erziehung des Menschengeschlechts kritisch und philosophisch erörtert, etc. Berlin, 1841, 8vo.

Gyurkovics, G. von.—Eine Studie über Lessing's "Laokoon." Wien, 1876, 8vo.

Haffner, P. — Eine Studie über G. E. Lessing. (*Görres Gesellschaft*, 1878.) Köln, 1878, 8vo.

Hammann, O.—Zur Rettung Lessings. Berlin, 1881, 8vo.

Hedge, Frederic H. — Prose Writers of Germany. Philadelphia [1871], 8vo. Lessing, pp. 81-98.

——Hours with German Classics. Boston, 1886, 8vo. Lessing, pp. 143-170.

Heinemann, H. — Shylock und Nathan. [Studies of the characters in the "Merchant of Venice" and "Nathan der Weise." Frankfurt a. M., 1886, 8vo.

Heinrichs, Ernst.—Ein Meisterstück Lessings oder Fragen und Anmerkungen zu Minna von Barnhelm. Hannover, 1870, 8vo.

Helveg, F.—Lessing og Grundtvig. Kjøbenhavn, 1863, 8vo.

Horn, Ferdinand.—Lessing, Jesus, und Kant, etc. Wien, 1880, 8vo.

Humbert, C.—Schiller, Lessing, Goethe, Molière, und Herr Dr. Paul Lindau. [Bielefeld] 1885, 8vo.

Jacobi, F. H.—Etwas das Lessing gesagt hat. Ein Commentar zu den Reisen der Päpste nebst Betrachtungen von einem Dritten. [By F. H. Jacobi.] Berlin, 1787, 8vo.

Jacoby, Johann.—G. E. Lessing der Philosoph. Berlin, 1863, 8vo.

Japp, Alexander Hay.—German Life and Literature in a series of biographical studies. London [1880], 8vo. Lessing, pp. 19-92.

Koepke, Ernst.—Studien zu Lessing's Nathan. Brandenburg, a. H., 1865, 4to.

Kayserling, M.—Moses Mendelssohn's philosophische und religiöse Grundsatze mit Hinblick auf Lessing. Leipzig, 1856, 8vo.

Klein, A. von.—Über Lessing's Meinungen vom heroischen Trauerspiel, und über Emilie Galotti. Frankfurt, 1781, 8vo.

Lang, H.—Religiöse Charaktere. Winterthur, 1862, 8vo. G. E. Lessing, pp. 215-304.

——G. E. Lessing. (*Profeten van den Nieuweren Tijd*, pp. 97-223.) 'S-Hertogenbosch, 1871, 8vo.

Lange, S. G.—M. S. G. Langen's Schreiben welches die Streitigkeit mit dem Herrn Lessing wegen der Uebersetzung des Horaz betrift. Halle, 1754, 8vo.

Latendorf, F.—Lessing's Name und der öffentliche Missbrauch desselben im neuen deutschen Reich, etc. München, 1886, 8vo.

Lehmann, A.—Forschungen über Lessing's Sprache. Braunschweig, 1875, 8vo.

Lehmann, Emil. — Lessing in seiner Bedeutung für die Juden, etc. Dresden, 1879, 8vo.

Lessing, C. G.—G. E. Lessing's Leben, nebst seinem noch übrigen litterarischen Nachlasse. 3 Thle. Berlin, 1793, 8vo.

Lessing, G. E.—Lessing, Bernardin de St. Pierre und ein Dritter. Eine Trilogie von Bekenntnissen, etc. Berlin, 1846, 8vo.

——Gotthold Ephraim Lessing. [Biographical and critical notice, with selections from the

666...66666.66666666666

works of G. E. Lessing.] Cassel, 1854, 16mo.
Bd. 47 of the "Moderne Klassiker."

——Die Feier von Lessing's hundertjährigem Todestage zu Braunschweig, etc. Braunschweig, 1881, 8vo.

——Lessings Vermachtniss. Reichenbach, 1881, 8vo.

——Randzeichnungen zu Janssen's Geschichte des deutschen Volkes. Ein Nachtrag zu G. E. Lessing's Rettungen. Frankfurt a. M., 1882, 8vo.
Heft. i., Bd. iv. of Haffner's "Frankfurter Zeitgemässe Bröschuren."

Lichtenberger, Frédéric. — La Théologie de G. E. Lessing. Strasbourg, 1854, 8vo.

Lowell, James Russell.—Among my Books. London, 1870, 8vo.
Lessing, pp. 276-329.

——The English Poets: Lessing, Rousseau: Essays by J. R. Lowell. (*Camelot Series.*) London, 1888, 8vo.
Lessing, pp. 261-310.

Maass, M. — G. E. Lessing's Erziehung des Menschengeschlechtes. Berlin, 1862, 8vo.

Marr, W.—Lessing contra Sem, etc. Berlin, 1885, 8vo.

Martineau, Harriet.—Miscellanies. 2 vols. Boston, 1836, 8vo.
Lessing's Hundred Thoughts, vol. ii., pp. 296-343.

Mayr, Richard.—Beiträge zur Beurtheilung G. E. Lessings. Wien, 1880, 8vo.

Melzer, Ernst.—Lessings philosophische Grundanschauung, etc. Neisse, 1882, 8vo.

Mendelssohn, Moses. — Moses Mendelssohn an die Freunde Lessings. Ein Anhang zu Herrn Jacobi Briefwechsel über die Lehre des Spinoza. Berlin, 1786, 8vo.

Michaëlis, C. Th.—Lessings Minna von Barnhelm und Cervantes' Don Quijote. Berlin, 1883, 8vo.

Michel, Karl.—Lessing und die heutigen Schauspieler. Hamburg, 1888, 8vo.
Hft. 34, 3 Jahr. of the "Deutsche Zeit-und-Streit-Fragen."

Modlinger, Samuel. — Lessing's Verdienste um das Judenthum. Eine Studie. Frankfurt am Main, 1869, 8vo.

Mohnike, G. C. F.—Lessingiana, etc. Leipzig, 1843, 8vo.

Muncker, Franz.—Lessing's persönliches und literarisches Verhältnis zu Klopstock. Frankfurt a. M., 1880, 8vo.

Murr, C. G.—Anmerkungen über Herrn Lessing's Laokoon, etc. Erlangen, 1769, 8vo.

Niemeyer, Eduard. — Lessing's Nathan der Weise durch eine historische - kritische Einleitung, etc. Leipzig, 1855, 8vo.

—— Jugendleben Klopstocks, Lessings, etc. Dresden [1868], 8vo.

——Lessing's Minna von Barnhelm. Historische - Kritische Einleitung nebst fortlaufendem Commentar. Dresden, 1870, 8vo.

Noetel, R.—Ueber Lessing's Minna von Barnhelm. Cottbus, 1880, 8vo.

Opzoomer, C. W.—Lessing, de vriend der Waarheid. Amsterdam, 1858, 8vo.

Pabst, C. R.—Vorlesungen über G. E. Lessing's Nathan. Bern, 1881, 8vo.

Pecht, Friedrich.—Lessing-Galerie. Charaktere aus Lessing's Werken. Leipzig, 1868, 4to.

Petri, V. F. L.—Worte der Weihe bei der Enthüllung der Lessing

Statue am xxix September
MDCCCLIII. Braunschweig, 1853,
8vo.

Pröhle, Heinrich.—Lessing, Wieland, Heinse, etc. Berlin, 1877,
8vo.

Rättig, H. — G. E. Lessing's
Bedeutung für unsere Zeit, etc.
Torgau [1881], 8vo.

Redlich. Carl C. — G. E. Lessing.
Festblatt zum 8 September,
1881. [Illustrations representing incidents in Lessing's life.]
Hamburg, 1881, fol.

Rehorn, Karl.—G. E. Lessing's
Stellung zur Philosophie des
Spinoza. Frankfurt am Main,
1877, 8vo.

Reinkens, Joseph H. — Lessing
über Toleranz, etc. Leipzig,
1883, 8vo.

Riehl, A.—G. E. Lessing, etc.
Graz, 1881, 8vo.

Riesser, Gabriel.—Einige Worte
über Lessing's Denkmal. Frankfurt a. M., 1881, 8vo.

Ritter, Heinrich.—Ueber Lessing's Philosophische und religiöse Grundsätze. (*Göttinger
Studien*, 1847.) Göttingen
[1847], 8vo.

Roennefahrt, J. G.—Lessing's
dramatisches Gedicht Nathan
der Weise. Stendal, 1863, 8vo.

Rötscher, Heinrich T.—Entwickel-
ung dramatischer Charaktere
aus Lessing's, Schiller's, und
Goethe's Werken, etc. Hanover, 1869, 8vo.

Rülf, J.—Lessing als Held der
Aufklärung, etc. Memel, 1881,
8vo.

Sachs, L. W.—Einiges zur Erin-
nerung an Lessing. Berlin,
1839, 8vo.

Sauer, August.—J. W. von Brawe,
der Schüler Lessings. Strass-
burg, 1878, 8vo.

Scherer, Wilhelm. — Geschichte
der Deutschen Literatur. Berlin, 1883, 8vo.
Lessing, pp. 438-470, etc.

——A History of German Literature. Translated by Mrs. F. C.
Conybeare. 2 vols. Oxford,
1886, 8vo.
Lessing, vol. ii., pp. 47-82.

Schiffmann, G. A.—Lessing's Nathan der Weise in seiner reli.
giösen Bedeutung. Ein Vortrag
Stettin, 1855, 8vo.

Schiller, C. G. W.—Lessing im
Fragmentenstreite, etc. Leipzig, 1865, 8vo.

Schink, Johann F.—Charakteristik G. E. Lessings. Chemnitz,
1795, 8vo.
Th. 2 of the "Pantheon der Deutschen.

——Charakteristik Gotthold
Ephraim Lessings, etc. Leipzig [1817], 8vo.

——G. E. Lessing's Leben, etc.
Berlin, 1825, 8vo.
There is a second title-page, which
reads "G. E. Lessing's sämmtliche
Schriften : ein und dreissigster
Theil."

Schmidt, Erich.—Lessing. Geschichte seines Lebens und
seiner Schriften. Berlin, 1884,
etc., 8vo.

Schmidt, H.—Études sur la Lit-
térature Allemande. I. Herder.
II. La Dramaturgie de Lessing.
Paris, 1869, 8vo.

Schumann, J.—G. E. Lessings
Schuljahre, etc. Trier, 1884,
8vo.

Schütz, C. G.—Ueber G. E. Lessing's Genie und Schriften, etc.
Halle, 1782, 8vo.

Schütz, F. W. von.—Apologie,
Lessing's dramatisches Gedicht
Nathan den Weisen betreffend,
etc. Leipzig, 1781, 8vo.

Schwarz, Carl.—G. E. Lessing als Theologe, etc. Halle, 1854, 8vo.

Seventornen, A. von.—Lessing in Wolfenbüttel, etc. Leipzig, 1883, 8vo.

Sierke, Eugen.—G. E. Lessing als angehender Dramatiker, etc. Königsberg, 1869, 8vo.

Sime, James.—Lessing. 2 vols. London, 1877, 8vo.
Part of "The English and Foreign Philosophical Library."

Spicker, Gideon.—Lessing's Weltanschauung, etc. Leipzig, 1883, 8vo.

Spielhagen, Friedrich.—Faust und Nathan. Ein Vortrag, etc. Berlin, 1867, 8vo.

Spörri, Hermann.—Rede bei der Enthüllung des Lessing-Denkmals in Hamburg den 8 Sept. 1881. Hamburg, 1881, 8vo.

Stahr, Adolf.—G. E. Lessing. Sein Leben und seine Werke. 2 Thle. Berlin, 1859, 8vo.

——The Life and Works of G. E. Lessing. From the German of Adolf Stahr. By E. P. Evans. 2 vols. Boston, 1866, 8vo.

Strauss, David F.—Lessing's Nathan der Weise. Ein Vortrag. Berlin, 1866, 8vo.

Taylor, Bayard.—Studies in German Literature. New York, 1879, 8vo.
Lessing, pp. 200-233.

Thimm, Franz. — The Literature of Germany, etc. London, 1866, 8vo.
Lessing, pp. 29-37.

Tolhausen, Alexander. — Klopstock, Lessing, and Wieland. A treatise on German Literature. London, 1848, 8vo.

Trosien, E. — Lessing's Nathan der Weise. Berlin, 1876, 8vo.
Heft. 263, Ser. xi. of Virchow's "Sammlung gemeinverständlicher wissenschaftlicher Vorträge."

Voss, J. von.—Der travestirte Nathan der Weise. Posse in zwei Akten, etc. Berlin, 1804, 8vo.

Wagner, B. A. — Lessing-Forschungen, nebst Nachträgen zu Lessings Werken. Berlin, 1881, 8vo.

Waldberg, Max R. von.—Studien zu Lessing's Stil in der Hamburgischen Dramaturgie. Berlin, 1882, 8vo.

Walesrode, Ludwig.—Demokratische Studien, 1861. Hamburg, 1861, 8vo.
G. E. Lessing, von F. Lassalle, pp. 475-505.

Walser, Jakob.—Lessing's und Göthe's charakteristische Anschauungen über die Aristotelische Katharsis. [Darmstadt, 1880] 8vo.

Weber, Theodor.—Lessing und die Kirche seiner Zeit. Barmen, 1871, 8vo.

Xantippus, *pseud.* — Berlin und Lessing. Friedrich der Grosse und die deutsche Litteratur. München, 1886, 8vo.

Zarncke, Friedrich.—Ueber den fünffüssigen Iambus, mit besonderer Rücksicht auf seine Behandlung durch Lessing, Schiller, und Goethe. Leipzig [1865], 4to.

Zimmern, Helen.—Gotthold Ephraim Lessing, his life and his works. London, 1878, 8vo.

MAGAZINE ARTICLES. ETC.

Lessing, G. E. — Edinburgh Review, by G. H. Lewes, vol. 82, 1845, pp. 451-

Lessing, G. E.
470.—New Monthly Magazine, vol. 100, 1854, pp. 127-137.—Nation, by E. E. Du Bois, vol. 4, 1867, pp. 66, 67.—Christian Examiner, by F. Tiffany, vol. 82, 1867, pp. 161-186.—Revue des Deux Mondes, by Victor Cherbuliez, vol. 79, 1868, pp. 78-121, 981-1024.—Fortnightly Review, by R. W. Macan, vol. 23 N.S., 1878, pp. 349-364.—Cornhill Magazine, vol. 38, 1878, pp. 189-206.

——*and Christianity.* Reformed Quarterly Review, vol. 27, p. 127, etc.

——*and his Works.* National Quarterly, vol. 12, p. 305, etc.

——*as Philosopher and Theologian.* British Quarterly Review, vol. 68, 1878, pp. 333-360.

——*as a Theologian.* Theological Review, by J. F. Smith, vol. 5, 1868, pp. 311-334.— Unitarian Review, by E. Zeller, vol. 10, pp. 377, etc., 469, etc.—Prospective Review, vol. 10, 1854, pp. 407-430.

——*Dramas of.* Nation, by F. Hall, vol. 28, 1879, pp. 154, 155.

——*Early Youth of.* Southern Messenger, by F. Schaller, vol. 14, pp. 253, etc.

——*Emilia Galotti: a tragedy; translated.* Democratic Review, vol. 22 N.S., 1848, pp. 511-518; vol. 23, pp. 237-246, 348-355, 421-431.

——*Grave of.* Every Saturday, vol. 9, pp. 355, etc.

——*Laocoon.* Blackwood's Edinburgh Magazine, by T. D. Quincey, vol. 16, 1824, pp. 312-

Lessing, G. E.
316; vol. 20, pp. 728-744; vole 21, pp. 9-24.—American Review, by J. D. Whelpley, vol. 13, 1851, pp. 17-26.

—— ——*New Translations of the Laocoon.* New Englander, by F. Carter, vol. 34, 1875, pp. 555-572.

——*Life and Works.* Westminster Review, vol. 40 N.S., 1870, pp. 442-470; vol. 53 N.S., 1878, pp. 91 139. — Foreign Quarterly Review, vol. 25, 1840, pp. 233-253.—North American Review, by J. R. Lowell, vol. 104, 1867, pp. 541-585.—Quarterly Review, vol. 147, 1879, pp. 1-48.—London Quarterly Review, vol. 51, 1879, pp. 425-448.

——*Minna von Barnhelm: a comedy; translated.* Democratic Review, vol. 24 N.S., 1849, pp. 176-179, 225-230, 345-354, 436-448, 535-546; vol. 25, pp. 56-67.

——*Nathan the Wise.* Edinburgh Review, by F. Jeffrey, vol. 8, 1806, pp. 149-154. — North American Review, vol. 106, 1868, pp. 704-712.—Retrospective Review, vol. 10, 1824, pp. 265-285.—Academy, Dec. 2, 1882, p. 391.

——*Prose Works of.* Nation, by F. Hall, vol. 29, 1879, pp. 196, 197.

——*Recent Biographies of.* Nation, by F. Hall, vol. 29, 1879, pp. 390, 391.

——*Stahr's Life of.* Littell's Living Age (from the *Saturday Review*), vol. 78, 1863, pp. 168-171.

V. CHRONOLOGICAL LIST OF WORKS.

www.ingramcontent.com/pod-product-compliance
Lightning Source LLC
Chambersburg PA
CBHW030110030726
47498CB00007B/2329